Ghost Boy of MacKenzie House

ACORNPRESS

P.O. Box 22024
Charlottetown, Prince Edward Island
C1A 9J2
acornpresscanada.com

Printed in Canada by Transcontinental
Edited by Marianne Ward
Designed by Matt Reid

Library and Archives Canada Cataloguing in Publication

Larsen, Patti, 1971-
Ghost boy of MacKenzie House / Patti Larsen.

ISBN 978-1-894838-71-9

I. Title.

PS8623.A7725G46 2012 jC813'.6 C2012-901105-3

The publisher acknowledges the support of the Government of Canada through the Canada Book Fund of the Department of Canadian Heritage, the Canada Council for the Arts Block Grant Program and the support of the Province of Prince Edward Island.

Ghost Boy of MacKenzie House

Patti Larsen

The Acorn Press
Charlottetown
2012

To all young writers who ever dreamed.
Yes, you can.

Chapter One

Chloe watched the men in the blue coveralls put the last of her bags in the back of the car, slamming the trunk with an echoed complaint of finality. She refused to look back over her shoulder at the neat two-storey that had, up until that moment, been her home her entire ten years of life. She didn't want to look because she knew if she did she would cry the whole way to Prince Edward Island.

Aunt Larry (short for Laverne, a name that always made Chloe's dad laugh) descended the steps behind Chloe, the solid clomp of her comfortable shoes sounding like approaching doom. Chloe knew what came next. Part of her wanted it, if only to escape the grief and disaster that her life had turned into. The other wanted to run back inside her old house, slam the door, and never come out.

"Ready?" Aunt Larry looked so much like Chloe's dad it made her heart hurt. Aunt Larry was tall, almost as tall as Patrick had been. Her hair was the same brown as his and Chloe's, her eyes an identical sea green. She even had their dusting of freckles across the nose. Chloe's skin was naturally darker because of her mom, Sophie, but otherwise she could have been Larry's daughter.

Chloe found she couldn't speak. Instead, she followed her aunt the last few steps to her hatchback and climbed in the back seat. The door thudded shut next to her—the soft breeze and hum of traffic on the highway a few houses over hushed to a muffled sigh. Chloe kept her eyes on her lap, locked on the slim silver bracelet that her parents had given her for her birthday, the last gift they would ever give her. She ignored the brief interruption as Aunt Larry climbed in the driver's seat, the silence returning with the closing of her door.

"Are you okay back there, honey?" Aunt Larry's eyes were the only thing Chloe could see when she glanced up at the rear-view mirror.

"Yes," she whispered.

The engine hummed to life. As they pulled away from her old life, Chloe had a moment of absolute panic. What if they weren't really gone? What if they were waiting for her in the house and she didn't see them because she wouldn't look?

Chloe pressed her forehead against the cool glass and stared at the empty silence of her living room picture window and felt the tears she struggled to keep inside pour out over her face. They weren't there. She was alone.

Chloe sobbed to herself for a long time while Aunt Larry passed her tissues over the seat.

It wasn't supposed to be this way. Chloe had the perfect life. Her mom, Sophie, stayed at home with her while her dad, Patrick, worked for one of the government ministers on Parliament Hill. Chloe never paid attention to which one. It didn't matter to her. Besides, her father didn't talk about work anyway, saying it was top secret and winking at her like he was a secret agent or something.

She had lots of friends, some of them from far-off countries, kids of diplomats who were in Canada while their parents worked at embassies in Ottawa. Chloe loved the activity of her street, the many kids who lived there, and the busy park at the end of her block where she spent a lot of her free time.

Life was wonderful and they were very happy.

Chloe snuffled back the last of her tears and blew her nose into a fresh tissue. She wadded up the soggy mess and stuffed it into the plastic bag Aunt Larry handed her.

"Feel better?" Aunt Larry asked.

Chloe shrugged. Her eyes were burning, her chest tight. She felt like she had run a dozen races in track and field without stopping, but worse because it was more like she was running from something rather than to something.

They stopped that night at a small hotel just inside the border of New Brunswick. She climbed into the queen-sized bed in the ordinary hotel room and tried to sleep over the sound of the air conditioner and Aunt Larry's snoring.

Chloe slid out of bed and went to her bag. She fished out a small photo of her parents and snuck into the bathroom. She sat down on the toilet, knees to her chest, hugging her legs while she studied the picture. She felt the now familiar burn of tears rising and the heaviness in her chest. She bit her lower lip and scrunched up her face to hold it in without success. The sadness passed, as did the tears, but it took quite a while.

Chloe went back to bed, holding her mom and dad in her hand under her pillow to keep them close, at last falling into a deep, exhausted sleep.

Chloe was feeling very alone that night when Sophie bent to kiss her forehead.

"Dad and I just need a night out to ourselves every once in a while," Sophie told her. Patrick kissed her, too, and they smiled at her as they swept out the door, Sophie's mocha skin glowing in the red dress she wore, Patrick handsome as ever in a suit and tie.

Chloe hated being left out. So when her babysitter Amanda asked her if she wanted to watch a movie, Chloe sulked and went to her room instead. She knew it wasn't right, but she wanted them to come home so much, she got herself worked up to tears. By the time Amanda found her, Chloe was crying so much she had made herself throw up.

"Baby, are you okay?" Sophie's voice was sweet on the phone. Chloe begged her to come home. She could hear the babysitter telling her parents that she was sick and hoped they listened.

"They're on their way," Amanda told her.

It took so long for them to get back, Chloe was dozing on the couch when Amanda got up and went to the door. Chloe could hear the heavy patter of rain on the side of the house as she dragged herself to her feet and went to follow, surprised to find Amanda with tears on her face and a grim police officer looking at her with regret.

Aunt Larry tried to stir up some excitement on the drive.

"Here's the bridge," she said, pointing in the distance. Chloe looked, feeling obligated. A thin grey line stretched out above the water as the Confederation Bridge that linked Prince Edward Island to the mainland rose up from the edge of the world.

"Cool," Chloe whispered, going back to her misery.

Still, as they drove across the huge expanse, Chloe felt herself perking up. She had never seen the ocean before. It was a deep blue, almost grey, with some greenish and white parts. Sea birds hovered over it while a sailboat bobbed and swayed in the distance. Chloe found herself straining to see over the edge of the railing, too high to catch more than glimpses now and then.

Aunt Larry must have noticed. "We're coming to the middle," she said. "The view is better. Look."

Chloe did. Stretched ahead of her was the rest of the grey ribbon they rode. The water went to the horizon on both sides. And in their path was the red shore of Prince Edward Island. Chloe watched the Island get closer and closer and felt Ontario get farther and farther away. As the car cleared the last of the bridge and drove back onto land, Chloe sat back and felt the sobs rise again.

Chloe was so confused. The officer was wrong. But Cliff and Laura Connell, Sophie and Patrick's best friends, arrived so Amanda could go home. Laura made Chloe pack a bag so she could go with them, but Chloe didn't want to go. She had to wait for her mom and dad. They would be home from dinner and Sophie would worry if she wasn't there.

It took Aunt Larry's arrival for Chloe to admit her parents were gone. That the car accident was real, that they were never coming back, and it was all her fault. She was sure her body would run out of water to make tears, but Aunt Larry told her as she crouched in front of her to hug her that she needed those tears to make herself better.

Chloe didn't think she would ever be better.

Aunt Larry worked fast. The funeral was small and

private, for which Chloe was glad. She wasn't sure how she ended up holding Aunt Larry's hand but she was grateful to have her there. Especially when the minister talked about how Sophie and Patrick were in a better place. That made Chloe sob so hard she thought she would die, too.

The only time she yelled at Aunt Larry was when she found out the house had been sold two days later. Aunt Larry listened to her with great calm and patience, then told Chloe she couldn't stay there by herself. Aunt Larry took her to the computer and showed her pictures of Prince Edward Island.

Chapter Two

Chloe didn't want to get out of the car. She knew she had to, but she was putting it off as long as possible. She kept her eyes down on her lap, on her fingers that twisted the slender silver bracelet around and around. The interior of the car was that mixture of hot from the sun and weird cold from air conditioning. She had a headache from it. Aunt Larry got out. The strange air in the car whooshed out the driver's door as she left. It got hotter than was comfortable, but Chloe didn't care. Getting out of the car, setting foot on Prince Edward Island for the first time, meant that it was all real and she was never going home again.

Her door opened on its own. Aunt Larry loomed, blocking the sun far to the west. Chloe caught the scent of her aunt's lilac perfume and thought of her mother.

"We're here, honey," Aunt Larry said. "Time to unpack."

Chloe nodded instead of speaking. Aunt Larry left her, but didn't close the door. Chloe could feel a soft breeze ruffle her brown bob. Sophie loved her hair. So much like her father's. Sophie's was black and curly and she was always fighting with it. Chloe wished for it herself, as well as her mom's soft mocha skin and chocolate-brown eyes.

Aunt Larry was talking to someone. Chloe let her eyes drift from the pebbled carpet beneath her feet to the view of the ground outside her door. Green grass waved at her. She could hear a humming sound, now that she was paying attention. It came and went in slow motion. Despite herself, Chloe looked up.

The sky was deep blue and very clear, starting to turn pink and red and gold along the edges of the west. The grass was vivid green, the driveway they sat on a deep, rich reddish brown like in the pictures Aunt Larry had shown her. A huge white house stood on the edge of nowhere, looking out over the blue ocean.

Chloe undid her seat belt and spun sideways. She dangled her pink flip-flops over the grass, debating. A soft yellow butterfly drifted toward her, settled on her big toe for a moment, then drifted off. Chloe let out her breath. She slid the silver chain around her wrist one last time and got out.

The grass was soft under her sandals. She took a step forward. The fresh air was nice after the confines of the car. Her headache was going away, even. Aunt Larry was speaking with one of the movers. Behind him was a younger man who winked at Chloe and tipped his ball cap to her, his back against the side of the white moving van. Chloe hugged herself and looked at the house. It had been freshly painted at some point, the white almost glowing against the deep black of the shutters. The front door was a lovely shade of green very close to the colour of the grass. Flowers bordered the small wide step that led to it. Just to its right was another set of stairs, these more modern, leading up to a deck that filled in the front corner of the house. The house was otherwise square, except for the third floor that was half a storey.

Chloe smelled lilacs again and spotted the bushes at the side of the house. Her mom's favourite. They had a bunch back home in Ottawa. Chloe shied from the memory of their split-level on their quiet street.

Off to the left, Chloe saw a farmhouse and a cluster of barns on the other side of a field. Turning slowly, she looked back the way they had come, as though she could see all the way home. Instead, she saw a big old barn, grey and weathered, and the winding red lane that went from the house on and on into the trees that bordered Larry's property before it disappeared on its way to the road.

Chloe continued her rotation. A freshly planted field of rich red earth ran along the trees across the upper corner of the property, beyond which was another field, overgrown with old weeds waving in the breeze. Further to her left, she spotted what looked like a decrepit cottage, just barely visible through the tall, swaying grass.

Aunt Larry was standing next to her when she finished with her circle. Chloe tried to smile, but it was hard.

"What do you think?" Chloe knew Aunt Larry was trying, had been trying since arriving in a hurry two weeks ago. She hadn't done much trying herself, but Aunt Larry understood.

"It's nice," she managed, voice soft. "I like your lilacs."

"Did you want to take a look around first?" Aunt Larry asked. "I have to tell the movers where to put your things."

"Okay," Chloe said.

Aunt Larry turned and pointed at the edge of the world that led to the water. "Just watch the cliff," she said.

Chloe wandered away from the car, hesitant at first. Not that she wasn't used to grass and fresh air, but it was different here. In Ottawa there were giant trees everywhere and lots of buildings. Neighbours were close by and you had to drive for hours to get to a lake to swim in. Chloe had never seen so much open space, felt such quiet. There were trees, but they were at the far edge of the expansive property. A row of big maples stood close to the house on the right, but otherwise the land was cleared. The lawn was huge and nicely cut.

She made her way along the left side of the house, drawn to the cliff and the water. Chloe ignored the lilac bushes with purpose and kept moving. She looked up as she passed the back part of the house, the big windows too high for her to see much inside. Chloe thought of her mom again. Sophie would love it here. She adored old stuff like this. Chloe bit her bottom lip hard to keep from crying.

The sea drew her onwards. The closer she got, the louder the humming became until it was a dull booming sound. The smell was amazing, fresh and tangy. It made her feel good. Chloe slowed as she drew close and crept forward as far as she dared. On the edge, she looked down.

The ocean was so loud! There were rocks below her, the waves throwing themselves against the shore. This was the source of the sound she had heard. She hadn't expected water to make so much noise. She had thought the surface was calm when she had seen it from a distance. Now she could see the whitecaps that gathered as the waves neared the shore. It was a marvelous sound. She could almost feel it through her feet as the waves hit the cliff. Chloe immediately loved the ocean.

The sun had begun its final descent. The sky in the west was a warm red and pink, and when she looked back toward the water, she saw that the deep red cliffs were glowing from it.

Cool, Chloe thought. Dad would love this.

She shuddered at the thought. Patrick's camera would be out, clicking and clicking as he captured every moment of it. She could almost see him beside her, laughing, eyes smiling. Chloe drew a wavering breath and looked away. When she did, her eyes caught movement below. She hadn't realized that there were kids on the rocks.

Chloe remembered Aunt Larry had said there were other kids around. She had expected to spend the summer alone. One of them looked up and saw her. He started waving. Without thinking, Chloe waved back. He scrambled away from the others and started up a rickety wooden staircase she hadn't noticed until that moment.

Chloe felt panic rise inside her. She wasn't ready to make friends or meet anyone. She wanted to go back to the car and close the door and have Aunt Larry drive her back to Ottawa and her old house and old friends. Chloe almost ran, but it was too late. By the time she was able to get her mind to connect to her feet, the boy was already there.

Chapter Three

He was a little taller than her and very skinny, his hands and feet filthy, stained red by the dirt. He was dressed in dark blue swim trunks, narrow chest heaving from the climb. He had so many freckles on his whole body that they almost covered him. Where he wasn't freckled, he was either very pale or bright red and peeling. His greenish-hazel eyes were fringed with red lashes, his hair the same bright orangey shade that reminded her of carrots. Chloe had never seen that colour hair before.

"Hi!" He bent at the waist, hands on his knees as he panted through his grin. "You're Chloe!"

She didn't move or speak. Turned out, she didn't have to. He went right on going.

"I'm Marshal MacKenzie, but everybody calls me Marsh. We live next door." He pointed across a field to the white house she'd seen earlier, surrounded by small barns and buildings. "Those are my brothers and sisters." He tossed his head over his shoulder at the other kids below. "I know about you because our mom and Larry are friends." He grinned with easy good nature, chattering on. "She told us you were coming here to live. Must be a big change from Ontario. Mom got us to look up where you're from on the Internet. She's been promising Niagara Falls ever since." He made a "yeah, right" kind of face as though used to disappointment. "I'm really happy you're here. There's nobody else around my age. Everybody is either older or younger. We're in the same grade!" His mind seemed to jump from thought to thought. Chloe felt overwhelmed by him but was grateful he was so talkative so she didn't have to say anything. "That's great! We can go on the bus together. I hate the bus, but it will be better if we're together." He seemed to be assuming they would be friends. He paused, head cocked to the side, shining red curls hanging over his eyes. She realized with a start he was expecting some sort of answer.

"Okay," she said.

That seemed to satisfy him. "Great! This is so cool, you coming in time for summer! It's the best time on the Island." He had the strangest accent. She almost missed some of his words because he talked so fast, but also because he ran them together in a bit of a slurred mumble. Chloe tried to keep up. "Not that you should be happy to be here. I mean, you should, but not for the reason you are." He flushed to the roots of his very red hair. "Darn. Mom said not to talk about it. Sorry about your parents."

Chloe didn't have time to feel sad. She found herself liking Marsh in spite of herself.

"That's okay," she said. "It was a car accident. There wasn't anything anybody could do." She had said it so many times in the last little while that it was beginning to sound like the truth. That part of her that knew she was lying still tried to get her attention, but Chloe found it easier to push it away. "It was two weeks ago." She found herself thinking it felt like a lot longer and yet as if it was that morning. "Aunt Larry was my dad's sister. Since my gram is ill... well, nobody else could take me."

"She's awesome," Marsh said with great enthusiasm. "Everybody loves her. Did you know she's been, like, everywhere in the world? Yeah, of course you do, she's your aunt. She tells the best stories about Africa and Asia and South America and helping people. I want to be a doctor like her and work in countries where people need help. Even the ladies at Women's Institute like her, Mom said, even though she's a CFA."

"What's a CFA?" Chloe asked.

"Come from away," Marsh grinned. "It's a thing, you know? If you're not born here, you're a CFA. You can never be an Islander, no matter what."

Chloe tried not to be offended. Who wanted to join their stupid club anyway? Marsh rambled on, oblivious.

"She bought the old homestead from my dad," he said.

"About five years ago. We all get along great. Do dinners and stuff together all the time. Guess you'll be coming, too, now."

Chloe shrugged. Before she could answer, they heard shouting. She joined Marsh in peering over the edge of the cliff. A tall teenager with Marsh's red hair was waving from below. He was shouting something, but Chloe couldn't make him out. Marsh, however, got the message.

"Gotta go," he said. "We're not supposed to be in the water after dark. Nice to meet you!" He was shivering in his wet bathing suit. Chloe noticed the temperature change as the sun went down. He started out across the lawn to his house. Chloe wasn't surprised when he turned back.

"I'll see you tomorrow, okay?"

"Okay," she answered.

She watched him run and hop through the field, thinking how odd he was and wondering if everyone on Prince Edward Island was like him.

The mosquitoes were out now. At least their whining buzz was familiar. Chloe turned and headed back to the house. She decided to finish her circle of the place, walking past the massive door facing the water and around the corner. A huge garden planted among the row of maples filled the side yard. She followed the tidy stone path through the banks of well-tended flowers, passing a small neat shed painted the same as the house. Chloe stepped up on the fresh wooden deck, the one she had seen from the front, which filled in the crook of the fat "L" shape of the house. The moment she did, she felt a shiver run through her.

Someone was watching her. Chloe looked around, but didn't see anyone. She looked into the house, but all she saw through the window was Aunt Larry talking on the phone in the kitchen. Larry saw her and waved for her to come inside. Chloe tried to shrug off the feeling, but it wouldn't go away. She took a slow step. As she did, the last of the sun caught the window above her, the only one on the smaller part of the house. Chloe looked up. The window was very small, the glass reflecting the sunset. She studied it for a moment. As she did, she was certain, even through the glare, that she saw a hazy face looking back at her.

Startled, she looked away. She had imagined it, she was sure. Still, it gave her the creeps.

Chloe stood there, frozen by the willies until Aunt Larry's voice calling her from indoors shook her out of her fear. With one last look at the window, Chloe went inside.

Chapter Four

Aunt Larry insisted on a tour of the house while the moving men got the last of the stuff placed where she wanted it. Most of the Suttons' possessions had been sold or given away in the last week, but there were certain pieces Aunt Larry wanted Chloe to keep, antiques Sophie had collected and intended for Chloe to have one day. Chloe went along with the tour, trying not to be interested. She didn't feel like she should care. But the big place was cool and she liked it right away, almost as much as the ocean.

Aunt Larry had restored and, according to her, improved the house. She told Chloe that when she moved in it had needed a lot of help to get it back to livable. Chloe admired the old stone fireplaces with heavy wooden mantels and big airy spaces with high ceilings and Larry's added touch of thick, white crown mouldings, all swirly and graceful. The kitchen was huge. Aunt Larry had installed an island in the middle of it. Big silver pots hung from a rack above it, with a fancy light in the middle. It was the only part of the house so far that felt modern, with shining stainless steel appliances and glass-doored cupboards she could see into.

The downstairs bathroom was big as well, just across the hall from the kitchen, with a nice, deep claw-foot tub. Chloe could almost hear Sophie having fits over it. It was so strange. They had intended to visit Aunt Larry, but hadn't gotten around to it. And now here Chloe was, living with her. It was all very weird and surreal and made Chloe feel funny inside, like she was dreaming and would wake up at any moment.

The strangest part of the house was at the front. Aunt Larry led her into a rustic room that felt different from everywhere else she had been. The walls were rough wood, unpainted. A big fireplace filled one wall, but wasn't ornamental like the rest. The mantel was scarred and scratched, the ends crumbling from age. The ceiling was supported by big, coarse beams. The floor was uneven and covered in cobbled stone.

"This was the original house," Aunt Larry explained. "In the old days, they would build a smaller place to live in until they had enough resources to add onto it. The family who lived here, the MacKenzies, became quite wealthy at one point. Everyone around here still calls my place MacKenzie House. Their farm was the most productive in the area, employing a great number of people. That's why the rest of the house seems so different. But they left the original as it was, so I did, too."

Chloe remembered Marsh. "I met a boy at the cliff. His last name is MacKenzie. He said they live next door."

Aunt Larry smiled and nodded. "Yes, that's right. Was it Marsh, already? He's been so excited to meet you." Her eyes twinkled at Chloe. "They are a lovely family, great neighbours, very friendly. You'll be meeting them all, I imagine, at some point."

"How come they don't live here?" Chloe ran her fingers over the rough stone of the fireplace and felt a creeping shiver climb up her back and across her shoulders.

Aunt Larry smiled, as if pleased Chloe was asking questions, showing interest. "I'm not sure," she admitted. "The family started having trouble and the farm was sold in parcels. I think it had something to do with a pair of brothers that lived here. Might be something we could ask Bill, Marsh's dad."

"Do you think he'll mind?" It seemed odd to Chloe to simply ask someone why their family lost their property, but Aunt Larry just shrugged.

"I doubt it," she said. "Honestly, I've never thought to ask."

Chloe was distracted by the return of that creepy feeling. That's when she noticed the stairs.

"This room was the living space," Aunt Larry said. "Up top was the sleeping quarters. It's fascinating if you want to have a look."

Chloe approached the stairs. They were boarded in from the living area, not open with a railing like a normal set of stairs would be. When she faced them head on, they formed a black tunnel up into the second floor, with an old-looking exterior door at her back. She glanced over her shoulder through the small window at the top of the door and spotted the lilac bushes at the side of the house.

She returned her attention to the stairs. The steps themselves were very worn—the wood bowed in the middle—and were quite steep and narrow.

"Where's the light?" Chloe asked, looking for a switch.

Aunt Larry laughed and handed her a flashlight from the mantel. "No electricity up there, I'm afraid. You can wait for morning, if you'd rather."

Chloe switched on the flashlight and aimed the beam up the steps. She couldn't wait. As reluctant as she was feeling, she had to go up.

Chloe started to climb. Her flip-flop caught on the third step and she stumbled. Aunt Larry was right behind her and steadied her. Chloe went on, braver with Aunt Larry there behind her. The beam of light lit the wall ahead of her and the low ceiling where the stairs ended. Chloe paused at the top and looked around. Right in front of her was a small window. The room was empty, old pine floors wavy with age. The ceiling was more beams, but sealed in this time. It was so small, she could barely imagine one person sleeping up there, let alone an entire family. Chloe took a step further, letting Aunt

Larry duck and follow her the rest of the way.

"This part of the house is really old," Aunt Larry said in a hushed voice as Chloe looked around. "About one hundred years if I was told right. The rest is younger, about seventy-five."

Chloe turned, the light hitting Aunt Larry. "Cool," she said, and meant it. The creepy feeling was still there, though.

"Ready to see the rest?" Aunt Larry was going down again. Chloe nodded, following her. When she approached the top of the stairs, a glint caught her eye. She walked to the window and looked out.

Below her was a clear view of the deck and the side garden. This was the smaller part of the house she had noticed from outside. She felt a shudder run through her. This was the window. Chloe spun, expecting to see someone behind her. But she was alone, really alone. Aunt Larry was gone. Chloe scrambled to follow, not wanting to be up there on her own even though she repeated to herself over and over as she stumbled down the slim, treacherous staircase that there was nothing to be afraid of.

The second floor of the newer part of the house was all big bedrooms, including Aunt Larry's. Chloe liked the massive mirrors and beautiful art everywhere, from paintings to tribal masks, fancy rugs, and weavings, all brought back by Aunt Larry from her travels. The two bathrooms on that floor were modernized. Chloe was grateful to see a shower.

At last, Aunt Larry showed Chloe to the third floor, what used to be the attic. At the top of a set of stairs was a narrow landing, with a door on one side and a hall on the other. The hall ended at another doorway, all chipped paint and warped wood. Aunt Larry saw Chloe looking at it. "Just old junk back there," she said before turning the white knob of the door in front of them. She stepped aside so Chloe could walk through first.

This part of the attic had been made over into a lovely bedroom, painted a soft yellow with windows on three sides. The ceiling was slanted on either side, making a cozy cubby for Chloe's bed at the far end, under a window. It was already set up, waiting to be made, her white and pink dressers and vanity slid into place.

"I thought you'd like it up here," Aunt Larry said. "We can put the furniture anywhere you want, okay?"

"Thanks," Chloe said.

"If you don't like this room, you can have one of the others." Chloe knew Aunt Larry was worried about her. Trying to mind her manners, she smiled a little.

"It's great. Thanks, Aunt Larry."

Her aunt beamed. "Wonderful! I'm glad you like it." Aunt Larry looked around. "I love this room, too. It feels like an adventure, somehow."

Chloe crossed to her bed and took a seat on the mattress. That surreal feeling came back to her as she did. Here was her familiar stuff all around her, things she knew well which felt like home but in a place that didn't. Chloe couldn't shake it.

"Can you believe it's this late?" Aunt Larry was looking at her watch, frowning. "Almost ten and neither of us has had a bite. I'm going to fix us something, Chloe. Come on down when you're settled. Your bedclothes are in this box." She deposited it beside Chloe. "We'll make it up after we eat, okay?"

Chloe nodded. "I'll be down in a minute," she said.

Aunt Larry left, and a good thing, too. It was all Chloe could do to hold back her tears until her aunt's footsteps echoed on the staircase. She grabbed a pillow and hugged it, crying with as little sound as possible. The house was nice but it wasn't home. The ocean was beautiful, but it was so different from what she knew. The boy Marsh was funny and odd and could be her friend, but she missed her old life. Chloe couldn't stand it anymore.

It was quite some time before she was able to go downstairs again.

Chapter Five

Chloe ate her way through the roast beef sandwich and small pile of potato chips Aunt Larry set in front of her. She kept her head down, hoping her aunt wouldn't notice the redness of her eyes. If Aunt Larry did, she didn't say anything. Chloe was grateful.

She liked her strange aunt and the way Marsh talked about her. Larry sent the best Christmas and birthday presents every year, stuff that amazed Chloe and made her feel like she was part of her aunt's adventures. But, despite that, Aunt Larry wasn't her mom or dad. Being single with no kids, she was sometimes as awkward around Chloe as Chloe felt herself.

"I know it's soon," Aunt Larry said. "But if you want to talk... we didn't get much of a chance. It's been so busy for both of us." Chloe noticed how tired her aunt looked and knew the accident had been hard on Larry, too. And she knew what her aunt meant. She flashed back to standing in the cemetery in her short black dress that Sophie bought her for their trip to the ballet that never happened. She remembered thinking the sun shouldn't be shining, that it should be raining outside like it was in her heart. She knew there had been other people around, but Chloe felt so alone, her and two cherry-wood coffins and two holes in the ground covered with fake grass blankets so no one would have to look at those holes.

Chloe snapped back to herself and realized that Aunt Larry was talking again.

"You haven't had any time to adjust, with the funeral and the sale of the house, now the move… I'm glad everything got wrapped up so fast in Ottawa, but I'm worried about you." Her smile was kind, Patrick's smile. Warm eyes, crinkled at the corners, a wide, full mouth. Straight nose, big jaw. If it wasn't for Aunt Larry's curly brown hair going grey, she could have been her brother. "I'm here for you, Chloe. For anything."

Chloe shut down the memories of the cemetery, of her parents, and everything that had happened. She ducked her head, fists tightening in her lap. She had lost her appetite.

"I don't want to talk about it," she said.

She heard Larry sigh. "Maybe you need to talk to someone else. I have a friend, she's great. Works with kids like you a lot."

"A therapist." Chloe spit out the words. She had heard the whispers at the funeral. From Sophie's friends and Patrick's. How Chloe should be in therapy, poor child. She hated the idea. How could a total stranger know anything about how she felt?

"Yes, Chloe. A therapist. You'd like her."

"I'm not going." She wasn't a rebellious girl, but the thought made her stomach clench and brought her headache back.

"Chloe... "

"I'm not crazy, I don't need a therapist, I'm not going!" She hadn't meant to yell. It came out of her and got louder and louder. Aunt Larry didn't get mad, though. She sat there with sad eyes and watched Chloe.

"Okay, honey," Aunt Larry said. "We'll figure it out ourselves."

There was a long silence. Chloe returned her gaze to her fists. She heard rather than saw Aunt Larry get up and shuffle through the kitchen.

"I got you something," she said as she rustled around in a bag before returning to the island where Chloe sat. "Every girl needs to read this, especially those who have just moved here." She slid something across the counter toward Chloe. She snuck a peek. A small soft-cover book looked back at her. It was trimmed in green, with a white house on the front. There was girl in a carriage with an old man. The girl had hair the same colour as Marsh's.

"It's a classic," Aunt Larry said. "I know you love to read. I hope you like it."

Chloe winced inside. It looked kind of dumb. Still, she felt bad for how she had reacted to Aunt Larry, so she tried to apologize by picking it up and reading the title.

"Anne of Green Gables," she said.

Aunt Larry was nodding. "World famous. I read it myself, when I got here. Marsh's mother gave it to me." She paused, hesitated, then spoke. "It's about an orphan girl who moves to PEI," she said.

Chloe almost threw the thing from her. The last thing she wanted to think about was what had brought her here in the first place. Aunt Larry should know better. Still, Chloe knew her aunt cared, so she stayed quiet, squeezing the book between her hands.

"Thanks," she said.

Chloe was anxious to contact her friends. She found her netbook, a gift from her father, in her travel bag and plugged it in. To her frustration, however, the old house had dial-up.

Aunt Larry laughed at Chloe's complaints. "You're lucky we have Internet at all," she said as she cleaned up their dinner. "Got it in about a month ago."

Chloe didn't care. After ten minutes trying to download her email, she gave up. Feeling isolated and angry, she snapped the thing shut.

"I'm tired," she said. "I'm going to bed, okay?"

"We're after time anyway, honey," Aunt Larry said. "Want me to help you make your bed?"

"No thanks." Chloe had been doing that job since she was seven.

"Sleep tight, then. Let me know if you need anything."

Chloe dragged herself up the two flights of stairs to her room, felt the heat of the day lingering in the upper floors, enjoyed walking into the warmth. She felt like the house itself was welcoming her. She rummaged for her toothbrush and some toothpaste and did a quick job of her teeth in the bathroom back down on the second floor. It was strange to see her toothbrush in the rack.

Like a vacation, Chloe thought. When we stay at hotels and stuff.

Only this wasn't a vacation and her toothbrush was going to be there for a long time.

Chapter Six

Chloe made short work of getting her bed in order. She tried not to remember doing the same job with her mom every Saturday morning and had to stop herself a couple of times from looking over her shoulder, half-expecting Sophie to be standing there watching her with a big smile on her face.

Her new room was a lot bigger than her old one, the slanted roof making her feel like she was in a giant tent, like in a story. She understood then Aunt Larry's reference to adventure. Being a world traveller, Aunt Larry must have stayed in places like this many times.

Once the bed was made, Chloe changed into her pajamas and switched on her favourite lamp before turning off the main light. The room was plunged into an odd half-darkness, the black pushing down against the little lamp. Chloe retrieved her flashlight from her bag along with her parents' photo and, with some reluctance, the copy of Anne of Green Gables. She snuggled under the covers. The window to the right of her bed, the one facing the ocean, was open to let in the nice breeze. She loved the smell of the Atlantic. She switched out the little lamp, burrowed under the comforter and sheet, and made a bit of a tent for herself. Once positioned, she turned on her flashlight. The cover of the novel and the shiny surface of the photo both winked at her. She was reaching for the book when she heard someone tapping at her window.

Chloe's heart leapt. She froze, listening. There it was again! She shivered, not wanting to look but knowing she had to. She peeked over the edge of the comforter, one eye clear. She checked the open window, but there was nothing. She looked at the opposite window. Again, nothing. This time when she heard the tap, she knew it was coming from the last window in the room, the one behind her. Chloe drew a deep breath and sat up, flashlight shining right at it. At first, she couldn't see anything. Then she heard the tap again. Something was out there. Chloe eased out of bed and snuck to the window. She quivered as she flashed the light outside.

A large tree branch waved in the breeze, the tip hitting the glass. It tapped at her a couple of times then swayed back. Chloe giggled with relief. She would have to tell Aunt Larry about it tomorrow. That branch had to go.

Chloe went back to bed. She had settled in her nest

when she heard a soft moaning sound. Braver this time, she investigated. Within moments, she was stuffing a stray sock into a tiny crack under the window to her left. Annoyed, she again retreated to her tent of covers.

She tried to ignore the occasional creak and groan from the house after that. It gave her the willies, but she knew there was nothing she could do about it. Instead, she opened the book and started to read. After a few pages, she admitted it was good, but she couldn't focus on it. She found herself rereading lines and even whole paragraphs because her mind wasn't in it. She slid the book out onto her bedside table and curled up with her flashlight and the photo.

Her parents smiled back at her. It was her favourite picture of them. They were both so happy. She remembered the day. They had gone to Lake Ontario for the whole week, stayed in Toronto for part of it and at Marsh's beloved Niagara Falls. That particular photo was taken outside the zoo. Chloe had been allowed to take it with Patrick's camera even though she was only eight at the time. She had wanted a picture of them and they had agreed. The next photo on the camera had been of all of them, taken by a nice tourist. But this one was Chloe's favourite. Her dad had given it to her when they got back, printed in his office on real photo paper. She loved how Sophie's curly hair had been blown to the side, flowing behind Patrick. The way her dark skin and Patrick's tan looked almost the same. How her dad's eyes sparkled in the sun, squinted in the corners because she insisted he take his sunglasses off. Sophie's right hand was outstretched toward Chloe, her left on Patrick's shoulder. Her father was laughing.

Chloe felt the tears well and fought them back. She hadn't begun this ritual so she could cry. This was her time with her mom and dad, her own time with no one else around to judge or call her crazy or tell her she needed a therapist.

"Hi, Mom," Chloe whispered. "Hi, Dad. We made it safe. Sorry I didn't talk to you last night but I had to share a bed with Aunt Larry and I didn't want her to hear us. She snores. Kind of like you, Dad." Chloe felt herself getting choked up. She hated the way her throat got tight and her chest heavy and her eyes burned. "I really miss you. It's okay here, but it isn't home. There are lilac bushes and old stuff. Mom, you'd love it. Dad, there's this big cliff over the ocean and it's red. It's cool. I'll take some pictures if you want." Chloe choked on a sob. "I just want to go home!" She tried to be quiet, not wanting Aunt Larry to come running. "I can't see you or visit you because you're there and I'm here. It's not fair!"

Tears ran from her eyes to her hair, tickling her ear. "Aunt Larry is nice, but it's not the same." She snuffled, wiping at her cheeks with the sleeve of her pajamas. "I did meet a kid, though. His name is Marsh. He talks funny, and a lot, like runs off at the mouth, Mom. He has red hair and a ton of freckles. He seems okay. It would be nice to have a friend here." All of her friends back home seemed so far away. She hadn't seen any of them since the night of the accident. Aunt Larry told her that their parents were trying to give her time, but Chloe knew the truth. They were protecting them, not for her sake, but from what had happened.

Chloe stroked her fingers over her parents' faces. "I love you," she said. "Aunt Larry said we can go back any time I want to see you. So that's okay, I guess."

Someone sighed. Chloe almost dropped the photo. She felt that same someone sit down on the edge of the bed next to her. It had to be Aunt Larry. She hadn't meant for her aunt to hear any of that. She pulled back the covers to apologize. As she did, the pressure beside her disappeared. And when Chloe shone her flashlight around the room, there was no one there.

Trembling, Chloe got out of bed and went to her door. She peeked out into the stairway, but it was empty. She held still, listening, and could hear Aunt Larry moving around the first floor far below her. She knew there was no way it could have been her aunt after all.

Not sure how to explain it away, Chloe went back to her bed and climbed under the covers. She switched on her bedside light and clutched her flashlight and the photo to her. It was a long time before she was able to fall asleep.

Chapter Seven

Chloe woke to the sound of birds in the tree outside her window and soft filtering sunlight that reached around the curtains to warm the end of her bed. She lay there a long time, still holding the flashlight and photo, and thought about what had happened. Certain in the light of day that she had imagined it, she tucked both items under her pillow and switched off her lamp.

The smell of breakfast drifted to her from the first floor. She followed the aroma through the quiet of the house to the wide staircase, her nose leading her all the way to the kitchen. She watched Aunt Larry from the doorway, feeling shy. It smelled great, like home. Her aunt turned and smiled at her.

"I take it you're hungry?"

"Yes, please," Chloe said, feeling hungry for the first time in two weeks.

"I hope pancakes will do it for you," Aunt Larry said, depositing two golden rounds onto a plate and pushing syrup and butter toward her. "Fresh bananas," she gestured with the spatula as she poured more batter into the pan. Chloe helped herself, slicing half the fruit over her pancakes before dropping on a dollop of butter and smothering it all in maple syrup. It tasted divine, chased with ice-cold milk.

"Good?"

"Yum!" Chloe smiled and felt it touch her heart. The pancakes were perfect. "Thanks, Aunt Larry."

Her aunt flipped two more onto a plate and offered them to her. Chloe wasn't about to say no.

She had made it through one more before Aunt Larry had her own ready and was debating another when someone knocked at the kitchen door. Chloe jumped, remembering the night before, then giggled to herself. Aunt Larry laughed.

"Gave me a start, too," she admitted. "Come on in!" The last was shouted across the room. Chloe giggled again. Sophie would not have approved. Aunt Larry winked at her as Marsh found his way in.

"Hi, Larry," he said. "Hi, Chloe." The screen door squealed shut behind him. Chloe smelled fresh air coming from him.

"Good morning, Mr. MacKenzie," Aunt Larry said. "Have you had breakfast?"

His eyes lit up. Very soon he was shovelling pancake and butter and syrup into his mouth while Chloe poured him some milk.

"What brings you by?" Aunt Larry was smiling, still at her own pancakes, though at a much more sedate pace.

Marsh almost choked, pointing his fork at Chloe as he gulped milk to clear the clog. "Came for her," he said. "Thought she'd like to have a look around."

Chloe looked outside. It was a beautiful day. The sun was shining, not a cloud to be seen. Full summer weather. Chloe had originally wanted to stay indoors where it was darker and gloomier to match her mood, but she was feeling a lot better now and was actually curious to explore further. She nodded.

"Okay," she said.

Moments after Marsh had cleared his plate with a swipe of his finger and had shoved said finger into his mouth to clean it off, he was dragging Chloe out the kitchen door, onto the deck, and down the path into the garden before she could say goodbye to Aunt Larry. Her aunt stood in the window and waved.

"Have fun!" she called after them.

Their first stop was the beach. Chloe found it scary going down the rickety staircase hammered into the rock. She was not fond of heights and was nervous when her flip-flops caught on the rough wood. She tried to keep up, but Marsh was a grasshopper, bounding his way down with abandon. He paused now and then to wait for her, then bounced over a few more steps, waiting like an eager puppy. Chloe was relieved when they reached the bottom. She was out of breath and her legs were weak, with a pronounced wobble from the steady descent.

Marsh, however, didn't give her time to recover. He pulled her over the warm red sand. The tide was further out than the day before, a huge bank of sandbars reaching far out into the water.

"The ocean is nice," she said.

Marsh snorted. "This isn't the ocean," he informed her. "This is the Northumberland Strait. Have to go all the way to the north shore to see the ocean."

Chloe was surprised. "Is it far?"

"Oh, yeah, super far, like at least twenty kilometres." He moved off as Chloe smiled to herself. She had to go that far to get to school in Ottawa. What odd people Islanders were.

The beach was a wonder. Natural caves were carved out of the soft sandstone in places. Up higher, seabirds dug holes in the cliff for their nests. Chloe stood and watched them for a while as they spun and danced above her before diving with perfect accuracy back home.

Marsh showed her where their family had a bonfire pit. They would come down sometimes and make s'mores while his father played guitar and they all sang. When Chloe asked how many were in his family she was stunned by his reply.

"Seven," he said. "Kids, anyway. Then there's Mom and Dad. Oh, and cousins and aunts and uncles. And Nanny." He rolled his eyes. "Tons of people. You'll meet them all."

Chloe, as an only child, wondered what it would have been like to have a brother or sister to go through her sadness with her.

Marsh didn't notice she was quiet. In fact, she was sure he was never quiet, so the fact he didn't even register her silence suited her down to the ground. "Trouble is, my brothers are a lot older than me and my sisters don't like to hang out. They like girl stuff too much." He made a face then turned to Chloe. "Sorry, um, I know you're a girl."

She smiled. "Yeah," she said.

"But you're cool," he said. "You know. Not a scaredy cat. Or whiny. More… "

"Thanks," Chloe said, knowing he was trying and deciding to give him the benefit of the doubt.

Marsh shrugged and grinned at her. "The sand bars are the best part!"

He dashed off into the water, leaving her to follow yet again. The water between the sandbars was very warm and full of life. Chloe wished she had worn her bathing suit, but at least her shorts were short enough to stay dry. Marsh showed her the tiny holes where clams lived and taught her how to make them squirt by stepping close.

They came across a crab. Marsh gave stern warnings while teasing the thing with a stick. He also told her about jellyfish (he called them bloodsuckers) and how their stingers could wrap around you even when it seemed they were far away. Chloe was losing her enthusiasm for swimming in the ocean. Too much stuff to think about.

By the time the sun was high, the tide was coming back in and Chloe was tired. She missed her sunglasses and was getting a headache from the glare on the water. With some reluctance, Marsh agreed to go.

"Not as much fun on my own," he admitted. She felt bad, but not enough to change her mind.

Marsh pointed to a second stairway, in no better condition, further down the beach toward his house. "I go that way," he said. "Hey, why don't you come home with me for lunch? Mom would love to meet you."

"Thanks," Chloe said, trying to let him down easy. The last thing she wanted was to spend lunch trying to make small talk with Marsh's mother. He was okay, but what if his mom wanted to talk about the accident? "I think I'm going to go home."

Marsh's face fell, but he didn't seem to take it personally.

"Okay," he said. "I'll see you tomorrow, though, right?" He was already off before she could answer. He waved and smiled so she waved and smiled back. She watched him until he reached the staircase before she headed home.

Chapter Eight

Chloe panted her way to the top of the stairs. By the time she reached the edge of the cliff, she was very tired. So tired, in fact, she collapsed on the grass for a minute to catch her breath. The stiff breeze that came in from the water cooled her as much as the earth beneath the thick grass. Between her toes was a great deal of the odd clinging clay that sat in sucking patches near the rocks and she had sand on her feet. She used handfuls of grass to wipe them clean. She found an outdoor faucet in the garden by the shed and used it to rinse the rest off, squealing at the ice-cold water. By the time she made it to the house, she was ready for lunch.

She knew by the quiet that Aunt Larry was gone. She checked the driveway through the kitchen window. Her aunt's hatchback hybrid was missing. Stomach rumbling, she moped to the island, trying to decide what to do. She was capable of making her own lunch, but this was the first time she was alone in the house and she wanted Aunt Larry there. She found a note next to the fruit bowl and did her best to decipher the terrible handwriting.

Gone to get some groceries and catch up on errands. Left you lunch in the microwave in case you didn't go to the MacKenzies' (figured Marsh would ask). See you this afternoon. Hope you had fun! Love, Aunt L

She had drawn a crooked heart in the bottom right-hand corner and filled it in with red pen. It made Chloe smile, dark mood and all. She went to the microwave and investigated. A plate of macaroni and cheese glowed at her. She heated it, poured another glass of milk, and devoured it all so fast it made her think of Marsh.

After lunch, Chloe debated what to do. Now that she was full and rested, she was bored. She sort of regretted not going with Marsh, but on the other hand knew he was part of the reason she was so tired. She again attempted to get her emails but gave up, leaving the computer on to do its work. She read a few chapters of Anne of Green Gables, finding herself giggling in places and feeling sorry for the girl in others, but felt restless. In the late afternoon, she put on socks and sneakers and went outside.

The cliff called to her. She went to the edge again. The water was in all the way, the waves lapping at the shore. It was quieter than the night before, but she could still hear the rush and sigh of it. Chloe started walking, the opposite direction from Marsh's. The wind was softer than it had been that morning, but still pushed her hair into her mouth from time to time. She came to the long, neglected grass as she left the property and was glad she had changed from her flip-flops. The cliff continued in a slight curve for what looked like miles. Lost in the sound of the waves and the smell of the ocean, Chloe kept walking, the tall green stalks slapping against her bare legs as she gathered handfuls of the soft tops to sift through her fingers.

When she encountered an old, rundown barbed-wire fence, she didn't think twice. It was so dilapidated she almost missed it, the toe of her sneaker meeting one of the fallen posts. It saved her from tripping and hurting herself on the wire. She hopped over and continued on.

Chloe paused to watch two sailboats in the distance. To her surprise, there was a big cruise ship out there as well, sailing into Charlottetown Harbour. Aunt Larry had promised Chloe they would go to town soon so she could look around and do some tourist stuff. Chloe hadn't cared at the time, but now she was curious. Maybe she would get a chance to see one of the ships when she was there.

Chloe was so wrapped up in her thoughts that she didn't hear the shouting until whoever was doing it was almost right behind her. She turned around in surprise to see an old man half-running, half-hobbling toward her. There was a small, once-white single-storey cottage behind him in the distance with a rusty car in the driveway. The man was the centre of her attention, however. He was very tall and slender, wearing dark blue work pants and heavy brown work boots. His shirt was the same colour as his pants, open at the collar, exposing a white T-shirt underneath. His grey hair was thin and longish, waving about him as he came roaring at her. He had a cane in one hand, but rather than using it to support himself, he was waving it at her. When he got close enough, she heard what he was saying.

"You git!" His face was very red, furious. He came to a thundering halt in front of her, panting and swaying, a terrifying figure hunched over her, blotting out the sun. "Git off my land! You're not welcome! I said git!"

Chloe was frozen, mortified, and afraid of the old guy. He waved his cane at her again.

"Trespasser! I'll be calling the cops, make no mistake!"

"But... " She could feel the blood rushing to her face as she got upset. Who was this guy? How dare he yell at her? Didn't everyone say how nice Islanders were?

"No trespassing!" He shook the cane again. It came very close to her, so close she flinched. "You damned kids, coming on my property, you aren't welcome, you hear?"

Chloe fought tears. No one had ever yelled at her like that before.

"Can't you see the fence?" He was spitting, he was so mad. Chloe looked back over her shoulder. The fence was in better condition as it moved up toward the cottage. Now that she was aware of it, that is.

"I'm sorry." Chloe took a hesitant step backwards.

He raised his cane menacingly over his head. "Git before I take this and tan your hide!"

Chloe took one look at the raised cane and ran.

Chapter Nine

Chloe ran all the way back to the damaged fence, not looking to see if he followed, hearing him shouting at her as she ran. She stumbled through the long, once gentle grass that pulled at her and made her trip and almost fall, tangling around her sneakers and ankles. She did fall, once, trying to get back over the barbed wire, catching one knee and her favourite shorts, tearing them in her need to get away. She hobbled on, even past his property, wanting to get home. She didn't realize she was angry until it rose up in her as sobs. By the time she reached the garden she was choking on furious tears, sweating from effort, ashamed and humiliated by how the man had treated her, and limping from the cut on her knee that left a trail down her shin to stain the top of her sock. She fingered the hole where the rusted wire had ripped her shorts and sobbed harder.

Aunt Larry flew out the back door. Part of Chloe was glad she was home while the other part wanted her to leave her alone.

"Chloe!" Her aunt gripped her shoulders. "What happened, honey?"

She managed to get the story out around her choking sobs. Larry was furious.

"That old crank," she said. "How dare he? You didn't know, honey. It's not your fault." Aunt Larry wiped at Chloe's tears. Knowing her aunt was on her side made Chloe feel better. "You just never mind Joseph MacKenzie," she said. "From what I hear he doesn't like anybody and nobody likes him, either. Oh, Chloe, I'm sorry. If I had known you were on your own this afternoon I would have warned you about him." Aunt Larry was very distressed.

Chloe swiped at her tears, sobs diminished to snuffles and the hiccups.

"I'm okay," she said. "He's mean." She hiccupped again. Aunt Larry hugged her. She smelled like Sophie, and kind of felt like Patrick, so Chloe let her.

When Aunt Larry let her go, Chloe felt better. And kind of silly for crying over it. She had a flash of the girl she was reading about and wished she was as brave as the red-haired Anne. She wouldn't have let the old man make her feel scared. She would have yelled right back at him. Chloe vowed to herself that would be the last time she'd let the old grump treat her the way he did.

Still, the upside of the whole business was she felt lighter than she had in two weeks. It was as if the scare had released the tension in her body, the same anxiety she'd been clinging to since the night of the accident, and it was all wiped away by her aunt's hug.

"I got us a movie," Aunt Larry said. "And stuff to make a pizza. Thought we'd have a night in and relax. Sound good?"

Chloe nodded and hugged Larry on impulse. Her aunt hugged her back. It was a long moment before Chloe stepped away.

"Did you get pineapple?" she asked.

Aunt Larry winked.

There was pineapple, Chloe's favourite, and hamburger, and some hot peppers for Larry's side, extra cheese and ham for Chloe's. While she had a shower and changed, Aunt Larry got going on the pizza. When Chloe came back downstairs, Aunt Larry paused in her cooking to examine Chloe's knee from her perch on the island. A little first aid and a Band-Aid later and Chloe was heaping toppings on her side of the pizza. As their creation cooked, Aunt Larry told Chloe about her most recent trip to Africa. Chloe was sad that Aunt Larry wouldn't be able to travel anymore because of her, but her aunt wasn't.

"Plenty of time for us to do some together," she said.

Chloe liked the sound of that.

The pizza was delicious, the movie funny. Even so, Chloe was going on little sleep and lots of emotion. About halfway through she couldn't help herself. She closed her eyes for a second to rest them and fell asleep.

Chloe woke in the dark curled up on the couch, a faded quilt draped over her and a knit covered pillow making an impression on the side of her face. The deep tolling of bells from the hall outside the living room echoed as the grandfather clock chimed twelve times.

Wanting the comfort of her own bed, Chloe kicked aside the blanket and padded her way to the stairs. As she mounted the first step, she heard a noise behind her. Startled, Chloe looked around. She didn't see anything or anyone. The sound came again, like someone sighing. It was coming from the entry to the old part of the house, with its creepy stairs. Chloe had no desire to investigate and ran the rest of the way to the second floor. She paused to do a quick job on her teeth, her eyes scanning the room behind her in the mirror as she did. The memory of what she had experienced the night before seemed far more real to her now that the house was dark and quiet.

She held her breath when she opened the bathroom door and made a dash for her room, trying to be quiet but hurry at the same time. She got into her pajamas and fell into bed, pulling the covers over her head, flashlight and photo in hand.

Chloe listened for a long time before peeking. She was alone. No sighing, no one sitting on the edge of her bed.

She retreated back under the covers and examined the photo of her parents.

"Sorry to be scared," she whispered to them. "I know it's silly and I imagined stuff last night. Maybe because I want so much to see you." Tears welled. She wondered how long they would keep coming. "Was it you, Mom?" The thought made her feel better. The idea that Sophie had perhaps come to comfort her lifted her spirits. "That would be cool," she said. "I wouldn't be scared then."

Chloe heard the sigh and felt the same pressure next to her. The fear returned, Sophie or no Sophie. But hoping maybe it was her mother after all, Chloe couldn't take the chance. She kept talking.

"Marsh took me to the beach today. It's awesome. Except for the crabs and jellyfish. He's funny, but I like him. Oh, and there's a mean old man down the road. He's horrible. He yelled at me for being on his property." Her anger surged back at the thought of Joseph MacKenzie. "Don't know what his problem is, and I don't care."

The sigh was louder this time. Chloe couldn't reason it away. Someone was there, sitting next to her. Taking her fear in hand, Chloe whipped back the covers, expecting to see her mom.

A softly glowing boy sat next to her, watching her.

Chloe screamed. He looked startled then vanished. Chloe shoved herself back as far as the headboard would let her and gathered her comforter around her, not even having the courage to turn on her lamp. She shone her flashlight around the room as her heart pounded in her chest. The boy was gone but her fear wasn't. She jumped when she heard feet on her steps and the creak of her door, and almost screamed again. But it was just Aunt Larry, looking sleep-tussled and bleary eyed.

"Chloe?" She came to the bed. Chloe reached for her. Aunt Larry sat and held her for a bit. "Nightmare?"

Chloe shook her head, shivering. "No," she said.

"What happened?" Aunt Larry was rubbing her back.

Chloe almost told her the truth. Almost. But something held her back. The word "therapist." Getting a hold on herself, Chloe leaned away.

"Sorry," she mumbled. "I thought I saw something, that's all."

Aunt Larry was frowning. "Are you sure you're okay?"

Chloe nodded, feeling miserable for lying and wanting to tell someone, but knew that Aunt Larry would worry and think she was seeing things because of her parents dying.

"Yes," Chloe said, voice still shaky with fright. I'll sleep with a light from now on, she promised herself. That made her feel better, enough that she was able to muster a smile for Aunt Larry.

Her aunt smiled back. "This old house has lots of creaks and bangs and noises, I know. It takes some time to get used to. Did you want me to stay for a while?"

Chloe did, but wouldn't admit it. "I'm okay," she said.

Aunt Larry went to the door. "If you need anything, come get me, honey."

Chloe kept smiling until Aunt Larry closed her door,

then dove back under her covers. As an afterthought, she snuck one hand out from under the blankets and turned on her brave little lamp. She lay awake most of the rest of the night with her flashlight growing dimmer and dimmer under her tent.

Chapter Ten

By the time Chloe managed to get herself out of bed (she had fallen asleep right around dawn), Aunt Larry had knocked on her door three times, twice for breakfast and the third to tell her she had to go out. Chloe was able to mutter something to satisfy her aunt and lay there listening as the front door thumped shut, the car door slammed, and Aunt Larry drove off.

Exhausted from two sleepless nights, Chloe cleaned herself up and got some cereal. Wanting to be out of the house, she took her glass and bowl out to the deck and ate in the sunshine. She sat with her back to the creepy window, trying to ignore it, but caught herself glancing over her shoulder at it more than once.

As she was finishing up, Marsh appeared around the

corner of the house. Seeing her, he grinned and waved. Feeling relief, wanting the distraction he would create, Chloe smiled and waved back.

"Morning, neighbour." He collapsed himself into the chair opposite her. "Sorry I'm late, had chores." He made a face. "The only thing I don't like about the farm."

Chloe had never been to a farm but guessed there were things that had to be done for the animals. Having never had a pet, even, she could only guess.

"What do you want to do today?" Marsh asked. "More beach?"

"Whatever," she said. "What is there to do?"

Marsh groaned. "That's the problem," he said. "Not much. Welcome to the Island. Boring is our middle name."

He was so dramatic, Chloe laughed. "There has to be something," she said.

"Beach," he admitted. "Farm. Read. Video games. TV. End of story."

Chloe was disappointed. Aside from the beach it sounded like home. The difference was, she was on her own. She was used to having Sophie to do those things with.

I'm not alone, she told herself. I've got Marsh.

"Okay, beach," she said. "But we have to stay away from the fence, okay?" She shuddered. "That guy who owns the other side is mean."

Marsh whistled, his eyes getting wide. "Tell me you didn't go over there."

"Yesterday," she said. "I went for a walk. Climbed over the fence." The memory was vivid and made her flush. She could feel her cheeks getting hotter and hotter. "He yelled at me."

Marsh nodded in sympathy. "Yeah, you got to stay away from him," he told her, voice hushed for no particular reason as his eyes drifted to the fence two fields away. "He's a real nutter, you know? Crazy." He leaned in closer. "We're related, if you can believe it. On my Dad's side. Joseph was Grampy's second cousin or some such. His family owned all this." He waved his arms, encompassing Aunt Larry's, the cottage, and his own family farm. "But bad things started to happen and the family fell apart. One daughter hung herself." He shivered. "Something to do with the war. Then the last two male heirs—Joseph and his brother—had this big fight, right? Split the whole family right down the middle." He punched his palm for effect. "There was too much land and a whole bunch of arguing, and when it was all over, the bank had to come in and sort things out. Dad said we're lucky any of the property came to us after all that."

If Marsh was related to the family who used to live here, Chloe wondered if he could help her with the ghost in her bedroom—if he'd even believe her, that is. She continued to ponder it as he went on.

"Anyhow, the bank had to sell off all the land, so that now there isn't much left. Dad inherited the new farm, and Larry bought the original homestead from us. All that's left of the original family is Joseph and the widow cottage where he lives. It's a shame, but like Dad says, farming isn't what it used to be. Could be even if the brothers hadn't fought, same thing would have happened, just slower. Lots of farms are gone now and no one is starting new ones."

Chloe thought he sounded like an old man talking that way. "So he's, like, some kind of cousin?" she prodded.

Marsh nodded, red head bobbing so fast his curls bounced. "Yup. Everyone is related here. First thing you get asked when you meet someone new is, who's your mom? Who's your dad? Where're you from?" He grinned. "Pretty soon you find out you're related on your mother's side through marriage or something."

Chloe thought it was funny. "Maybe you could show me the farm?" Getting away from the house for a while sounded like a good idea.

Marsh lit up. "Sure!" He was on his feet and moving before Chloe knew what happened. "Coming or not?"

After a brief visit to the kitchen to put her dishes in the dishwasher, Chloe followed Marsh across the field to his house.

"Nobody plants in this one anymore," he told her over his shoulder as she struggled to keep up. He noticed and slowed his headlong plunge through the tall grass.

"How come?" Chloe was having more trouble than him and hoped keeping him talking would slow him down.

"Not enough money in it," he told her. "And Dad doesn't have time anymore. The tractor is fine for small jobs but we don't have the right equipment. Some farmer from up west wanted to rent it for potatoes, but your Aunt Larry said no. Didn't want all the chemicals so close to the house."

Chloe realized there was a lot more to farming than she had thought.

By the time they reached the edge of the field she was dusty and sweaty and feeling unhappy about the whole business. She had been forced to dodge bees and other nasty critters, and felt a mouse run across her foot once, making her jump and squeal. Marsh didn't notice, however, and picked up the pace across the grass behind his house. The going was easier at least. Chloe did her best to keep up.

They were greeted by a giant white dog with a thick, furry coat. He ran at them, barking. Chloe hesitated as the dog tackled Marsh. She felt better when he licked the boy's face rather than biting him before trotting up to her and shoving his big head under her hand for a scratch.

"Don't worry about Shep," Marsh said. "He won't hurt a fly, let alone the coyotes we want him to chase." Shep was drooling on Chloe's foot but she didn't mind. He joined them as they took the tour.

Most of the small buildings were empty and worn-looking, down to bare wood if they had ever been painted at all. A few looked like they were ready to fall in. Marsh showed her the grain silo, a short, round building made of steel with a funny pointed cap. She peeked her head inside and smelled dust, amazed at the big pile of shining yellow grain inside. Marsh took a handful and held it out to her. It tickled her hand as it trickled through her fingers.

Next was the chicken coop. The chickens were kind of cute but the whole place had a nasty odour so they didn't stay long. The cows were better since they were out in the field, but Marsh informed her she didn't want to go into their barn because it hadn't been cleaned out in two weeks. She giggled as one of the reddish brown cows with a solid white face accepted a clump of grass from her hand and let her scratch its wide forehead. Shep exchanged a nose touch with the same cow then went and flopped himself down in the shade of a maple tree.

To Chloe's delight, they also had horses. Well, a pony, at least, named Pretty Girl, all dappled grey with a long mane and tail, and a big draft horse the same colour. Marsh told her he was a Shire and his name was Whisper.

"I love horses," Chloe said, holding her hand out.

"Whisper's great," he said. "He's really old and nice. But Pretty Girl is nasty."

As if to agree with him, the pony snapped at Chloe's fingers and trotted off. Shep barked at her and chased her around the field. Chloe felt like cheering him on.

"It's not a real farm anymore," Marsh admitted as they made their way to the house, Shep walking along beside. "The chickens and cows were supposed to go in the freezer, you know, for food." Chloe was horrified. She never thought about where meat came from. A small white chicken ran past her, chased by another, this one a shade of brown. The idea of eating them made her queasy. She swallowed hard as Marsh went on. "My Dad is an accountant." He said it like an apology. "He was raised on the farm but never did any of that stuff himself. And we got so attached to the animals that they're all pets now." Chloe felt better immediately.

They paused at the farmhouse long enough to get a drink. Chloe thought it felt a lot like Aunt Larry's except more careworn and without the cool stuff. Plus, the house was a bit of a mess. She had to make a spot on the crowded counter to place her used glass after finishing her lemonade.

When they went out the kitchen door, she heard shouting and laughter coming from the other side of the yard. They followed the sound to find Marsh's brothers and sisters playing by a small pond. It was oval-shaped, backed by a thick patch of bulrushes. Chloe could see a track leading away from the pond headed for a marsh off in the distance. She returned her attention to the kids and found them all staring at her.

They all had the same red hair and freckles, but in varying degrees. Two of the boys, teenagers Chloe guessed, looked so much alike they had to be twins.

"Lucas and Logan," Marsh said.

They waved at the same time and went back to whatever they were doing, hanging over the edge of the pond, their shorts filthy and soaked through.

The oldest boy she remembered from the first day. "I'm

Liam," he said. "Nice to meet you, Chloe. Marsh driving you nutters yet?"

Marsh rolled his eyes at his brother while the oldest girl giggled. She was cross-legged on the ground, a little girl in her lap. Her long red hair was pulled back in a ponytail. She was much neater than her brothers and even had nail polish on.

"I'm Rebecca," she said. "This is Olivia," she pointed to the little copy of her that sat between her legs, looking at Chloe with huge eyes while she chewed on a dandelion, "and that is Gracie." A second, also younger girl was rolling in the grass with the happy Shep. Chloe couldn't believe how much they all looked alike.

"Hi," she said.

"Like PEI so far?" Rebecca took the flower from her sister who picked another.

"It's okay," Chloe answered, feeling shy.

"Yeah, but it can be weird, too. My best friend is from Ontario, moved here last year. She had the hardest time." Rebecca laughed. "But she's okay now."

Chloe smiled back, liking all the kids already. Best part was, at least some of them were more normal.

"Been to the barn yet?" Lucas or Logan, Chloe had no idea which was which, grinned at her like it was some big joke. The other twin joined in while Rebecca threw a small clump of grass at them.

"Leave off, you two," she snapped. "Ignore them, Chloe. They're idiots."

Chloe, however, was curious.

"Which barn?" she asked. The farm had so many.

The second twin (Logan, she decided) got up and pointed. Chloe could see the pale grey roof of the big old barn she had forgotten was in Aunt Larry's yard.

"MacKenzie Barn," he said. "Been around forever. Has the best loft."

Chloe was confused. "Why's that?"

"For jumping," Lucas said, still on the ground. "Dad put a new pile of grain in there for storage."

The thought of jumping from a loft didn't sound like a whole lot of fun to Chloe.

"We were heading over," Logan said. "Is Larry gone?"

Chloe nodded. The twins lit up. Lucas leapt to his feet and took off, followed immediately by Logan. Rebecca hollered after them to get their butts back, but they didn't listen. She got to her feet, scowling at Liam for not doing anything about them.

"I guess I'll have to go get them," he said, grinning. Rebecca wrinkled her nose at Chloe while Marsh followed his brothers, also beaming.

"Boys," she said. "You want to stay here?"

Chloe hesitated. She liked Rebecca, but the girl was older than her, and Chloe didn't feel like babysitting the two restless kid sisters she had with her.

"I guess I'll go home," Chloe told her.

Rebecca waved. "Nice meeting you, Chloe." Gracie offered her own enthusiastic, bouncing goodbye while Olivia ignored them all, absorbed in the dandelions.

Chloe made it to the edge of the property and headed

into the long grass again. She had every intention of going back to the house but the laughter she heard ringing from the old grey barn made her pause. Curiosity getting the better of her, she decided to check it out after all.

Chapter Eleven

MacKenzie Barn was a large, hulking building, the front doors two flat panels hooked together by a piece of wood that swiveled on a nail. One of them hung open. Chloe peeked inside. It was gloomy but not dark, the air full of dust and the smell of old dirt and autumn. Chloe stepped inside and almost leapt out of her skin as Marsh yelled, "Cannonball!"

He flew through the air, landing with a hiss in a giant pile of yellow grain, half-burying himself in the stuff before slithering down the side of the pile, shaking the bits from his hair. Chloe sneezed as the dust he raised reached her.

"You got to try this!" He grinned at her, pulling her toward a row of boards nailed to the far wall. They were as worn as the outside of the place, thick with old cobwebs that glowed white in the dim sunlight that filtered through the filthy windows. Chloe hesitated but found herself being boosted up onto the first board and felt she had no alternative.

She made it up three steps of the makeshift ladder before glancing down. Her world wobbled as she swayed there, terrified but unable to retreat. Marsh was right behind her. Chloe was forced to continue on up into the dark of the attic. She reached the last board and felt hands reach for her, pulling her up through the hole and onto the rattling, splintered floor of the loft. She shivered despite the heat in the huge, domed area, afraid to look over the edge of the hole to the ground below. She backed up a few steps and hugged herself, watching Marsh scramble up by himself to stand beside her.

His eyes shone in the low light, teeth flashing. "It's way fun," he said with great enthusiasm. "A little scary the first time, but you'll get the hang of it. Come on, it's your turn!"

Chloe held back, however, watching as first Liam, then the twins, made fantastic leaps into the air, plummeting out of sight. She knew they were all right from the encouraging comments but wasn't ready to try it herself.

"Geronimo!" Marsh spun past her, a huge grin on his face, dropping fast into the soft pile, sending up a cloud of dust. He coughed on it but he was laughing, so she knew he was okay.

She could hear the soft cooing of pigeons far above and looked way up to the peak of the hip roof, curving into the darkness. The loft was very quiet with all four brothers below.

"Chloe!" Marsh called. "Come on!"

She eased her way to the edge of the hole and looked down. The lower part of the barn seemed bright in comparison, the top of the grain pile very far away. She drew a shaking breath as the brothers all shouted their encouragement.

"You can do it!" "Just jump!" "Don't think about it!" "It's fun, honest!"

Chloe glanced over at the top of the board ladder and considered climbing down. But to get to it she would have to sit on the edge of the hole and stretch her legs to reach the ladder on the other side. She was afraid she would fall. Besides, she didn't want her new friends to think she was chicken.

Telling herself it couldn't be so bad if the boys managed it, Chloe drew a shaking breath and slid her sneakers to the edge of the hole. She planned to close her eyes and drop, not willing to attempt any of the crazy jumps the MacKenzies had, but as she decided to let herself go, she heard someone gasp.

Chloe spun and saw the ghost boy standing behind her. His face was full of fear, hands reaching for her. She started and moved away from him, then felt her feet slip on the edge of the hole. She twisted and fell in slow motion, eyes locked on the boy as she plummeted to the ground.

Chloe panted for the breath that had left her after she

hit the grain pile. She was surrounded by red heads and freckles as the boys hovered, looking anxious.

"Chloe," Liam said, "are you okay?"

She tried to find the ghost, but he had vanished. Her lungs began to work and she choked and coughed on the dust. Liam and Marsh helped her sit up, Marsh pounding her on the back.

"I'm okay," she wheezed at last. "I slipped."

"You scared us," Liam said, laughing.

"I scared myself," she admitted.

They all heard the rumble of tires on dirt as Aunt Larry's car drove by, headed for the house. The twins were up and running, not even saying goodbye as they dashed out the door and disappeared.

Liam scowled after them, then helped Chloe to her feet. She patted at her clothes, full of chaff, feeling the kernels grind around in her sneakers and socks.

"We need to get out of here before we get in trouble," Marsh said.

Chloe followed the brothers to the door and paused behind them, waiting until they slid outside to do so as well. Liam closed the door, spun the wooden block sideways to barricade the entry, then waved and left for home.

Marsh was sitting on the grass, dumping grain from his shoes. Chloe followed suit. She discovered while she slid off her second sock that her silver bracelet was gone.

"It can't be!" She got to her feet and looked at the barn. "It has to be in the grain!"

Marsh looked instantly distressed. "What did you lose?"

"My bracelet." She found herself crying. The scare and the ghost sighting paired with the loss of her last connection with her mom and dad made everything well up again.

"We'll find it," Marsh said, patting her shoulder to make her feel better.

They snuck back inside and spent the next hour sifting through the grain. At last, Chloe gave up, unable to see much through her tears and sneezes.

Dejected, she dragged herself home, leaving Marsh behind without even a goodbye.

Aunt Larry took one look and sent her right to the shower. Chloe was grateful that her aunt didn't ask too many questions. She went to bed after making herself eat something. Her appetite was gone with the bracelet and not even the memory of the boy in the loft could shake her loose from her grief.

She spotted her parents' picture and dragged it to her.

"Why did you have to die?" she asked them. "Why did you have to leave me? It's all your fault!" Chloe threw the picture away but went scrambling after it, retrieving it almost before it settled on the light pink rug beneath her bed. She smoothed it with her fingers before kissing both of her parents' faces.

She spent the next few hours feeling sorry for herself. Rather than suffer alone, she picked up the copy of Anne of Green Gables again. In between reading came bouts of more crying. The further she read, the more connected she felt to Anne. Life seemed very unfair to the fictional redhead, much as it did to Chloe. By the time it got dark, she had cried so much her eyes were sore and her throat ached like she had a cold, and she had a slight headache from focusing on reading through all those tears. She was tired, but couldn't sleep. A warm breeze was blowing in from her oceanside window. Chloe sat in front of it and breathed in the salt air. As she did, she felt a powerful compulsion to go outside. She took her parents' picture and her flashlight and crept down the stairs and out the back door without meeting Aunt Larry. She ran through the garden in her bare feet and all the way to the cliff where she sat on the edge, legs dangling over.

Chloe held up the picture and pointed it at the water. "See?" she said to her parents. "That's the Northumberland Strait. And the beach. See the cliffs, Dad?" It was so dark, she could only see the tops of the waves as they rolled, white and frothy, against the rocks beneath her. "This is where I live now. This is where I live." She was so sure she had no more tears, and yet there were more, and more after those. She was sobbing again, hurting so much but not able to find a way to feel better.

Aunt Larry sat down next to Chloe and tried to put her arm around her. Chloe jerked away, not wanting to be comforted.

"Leave me alone," she snapped.

"I want to help you," Aunt Larry said. "Please, Chloe, let me help."

"You can't help!" Chloe got to her feet. "They're dead! How can you help dead?"

Aunt Larry didn't move. She looked very sad but Chloe didn't care. "I can't," she said. "But you're still here, honey."

"Yeah," Chloe said, putting all her hurt and embarrassment and anger into her words to her aunt, all the while knowing she didn't deserve it. "I am. I just want my mom and dad and to go home, but I'm stuck here with you!"

Aunt Larry flinched. Chloe immediately felt horrible but didn't know how to fix it. She didn't think saying she was sorry was enough. Sophie would have been furious with her.

Lost and feeling very much alone, Chloe ran back to the house and to her room. She crawled into bed, trying not to hear the sounds of Aunt Larry closing up the house for the night. It wasn't until she heard her aunt's bedroom door close through the floor beneath her that Chloe thought of the ghost boy. Her heart tried to race but she was so tired. She peeked out once. He was nowhere in sight. Chloe fell into a restless sleep before she could check again.

Chapter Twelve

Chloe hesitated at the kitchen door the next morning. Aunt Larry was making breakfast. Chloe had been able to smell the salty bacon all the way from her attic room.

Aunt Larry greeted her with a smile and a full plate of food. Chloe said a quiet thank you and sat down to eat, grateful her aunt wasn't angry, but still feeling bad about the way she had treated her. She was so intent on her meal she was startled by a low rumble in the distance.

"Storm coming," Aunt Larry said. "Weather network says lots of rain. Check your windows after breakfast, okay, Chloe?"

When they were finished eating, Chloe helped Aunt Larry secure the house. It consisted of her following her aunt around from room to room while Aunt Larry closed the windows, but Chloe felt like she was helping somehow so it made her feel better.

"I'm working this morning," Aunt Larry told her. "I'll be in my office if you need me."

Chloe's heart fell. Aunt Larry was mad at her after all. Her aunt must have sensed what Chloe was thinking because she smiled.

"You can help me with my files if you want," she said.

Chloe hugged her hard as an apology. She spent the next hour filing away the slim yellow folders that Aunt Larry handed her out of a big cardboard box.

"I've been meaning to do this for a while," her aunt said. "These are my case files from my last trip to Mozambique." She let Chloe open one. She admired the beautiful tribal boy with his tattoos and unusual dress in the picture attached to the medical sheet. "I keep meaning to sort these and write a paper, but..." Aunt Larry trailed off with a laugh. "Maybe I'll have time, now."

Filing done, there wasn't much for Chloe to do. She left Aunt Larry to her work and drifted into the main part of the house, closing the office door behind her.

She jumped when she heard the first drops of rain hit the windows. They were huge, fat drops that made heavy splat sounds, a few at first, then more and more as the sky got very dark and opened up. Chloe was breathless. The whole house vibrated with the rain, it seemed, the sound of it drowning out everything. Chloe stood frozen until banging on the kitchen door shook her out of it. She ran to open it and found Marsh standing there, soaked through, rain dripping from his ears and the tip of his nose, his red curls plastered to his face. He held up a bunch of wildflowers in one hand, several of which were bent to the side, stems broken.

"I'm sorry," he said.

Chloe took pity on him. "It's okay," she answered. "Come on in."

Two towels later and he was pretty much dry. Chloe was putting the poor flowers in a glass of water when Aunt Larry poked her head out long enough to smile at them before going back to work.

"Some rain, huh?" Marsh was back to his old grinning self.

"Yeah," Chloe said.

"So what do you want to do?" He perched himself on one of the bar stools at the kitchen island, bare feet swinging. "TV will be kind of messed up because of the thunder and lightning." In answer, more thunder rumbled overhead. This time it was dark enough from the sullen cloud cover that Chloe caught the flash of lightning that preceded it. "Same for dial-up Internet. Got any games?"

Chloe wasn't sure. Aunt Larry would know, but she didn't want to disturb her again.

"Ever play rummy?" Marsh fished a beat-up old deck of cards from his pocket. Chloe hadn't and, intrigued, let him teach her. It became apparent to her that she was a sore loser. She tried not to complain too much but when she lost she thought the game was dumb. However, the more she huffed, the more she won. When she figured out Marsh was letting her win, she laughed.

She had a good hand and was about to put herself out when she heard a noise like a sigh from behind her. Chloe jumped so much she knocked over her glass of water and had to run for a tea towel to clean up the mess. She looked over her shoulder a few times, nervous again. It was dark enough from the storm clouds that the ghost boy could make an appearance.

"What's up?" Marsh asked.

Chloe almost didn't tell him. But she needed to share it with someone and he was her only option.

"You can't think I'm crazy," she whispered to him. Marsh perked up.

"Promise," he whispered back.

Chloe shivered. "I've been hearing, you know,... noises."

"Yeah?" Marsh was all ears.

"And feeling like, I don't know, someone is... watching me."

His eyes were huge. "Yeah?"

"And the other night... I was going to sleep... " There was no way she was telling him she talked to her parents every night so she glossed over that part. "I heard this sigh, you know? And felt someone sit down on the bed."

"Beside you?" Marsh's voice squeaked.

Chloe nodded. "Right beside me. So I looked."

"And?" He swallowed hard.

"There was... " She hesitated. She had him. It would be easy to pretend she was pulling a joke on him. She was sure his brothers did it to him all the time. But he believed her so far and she needed someone to. So, she took the plunge.

"There was a boy sitting on my bed."

Marsh let out his breath in a whoosh of air. "No way! What did he look like?"

Chloe was so grateful he believed her without hesitation that she told him everything. "He was kind of glowing, you know? I think he was our age." She frowned to herself, trying to remember details. She had gotten a better look at him in the loft than the night before in her room. But she had been so afraid she didn't remember much.

"What was he wearing?" Marsh asked.

"Um... dark pants, white shirt. It had a collar, I think. And suspenders. He had... dark hair. I don't know," she admitted. "I was so scared I don't remember a whole lot else. Except, he looked really sad." He had, she remembered that clear as day. Like he had been crying, too.

"Cool," Marsh said. "So cool. You know what?"

"What?" Chloe asked.

"I've seen him, too," Marsh said.

Chloe was shocked. "Really? When?"

"Two summers ago," he told her, leaning closer, glancing at the door to Aunt Larry's office. "Larry was in Africa or something and we were looking after the house, just checking on it, you know? I was here with my Dad," he added, "so I wasn't snooping. Anyway, I went around the back to check the door and I felt like someone was watching me." He shivered like Chloe had but he was grinning. "It was freaky! I looked up at the little window, you know, the one above the deck? There was this boy up there looking down at me."

Chloe realized she was holding her breath. "And?"

Marsh leaned back and shrugged. "I freaked. Went running for Dad. I was a kid, you know, only eight. Thought the bogeyman was coming to get me." He was laughing and Chloe joined in, even though it didn't feel funny to her. It was so much easier to be brave with Marsh there with her.

"Anyway, Dad came with me and had a look, but the boy was gone. Never saw him again. Of course, it doesn't keep Liam and the twins from torturing me." Marsh made his funny face. "Dad told them all at dinner and they started calling me the ghost hunter." He was blushing, ducking his head as if he expected her to laugh at him.

"Well, he's real," Chloe said. "So I believe you."

Marsh's smile lit up the room.

"I have a great idea," he said. Chloe was sure she wouldn't agree, but let him talk. "I say we go up to that room where the window is and see if we can find him."

Chloe did not want to go up there. In fact, everything in her wished she had kept her mouth shut. But Marsh was smiling at her, so eager and excited that she found herself saying words she couldn't believe were coming from her mouth.

"I'll get the flashlight."

Chapter Thirteen

Chloe's decision was a huge surprise to her, as was finding herself in the kitchen retrieving a second flashlight after Marsh claimed the one on the mantel in the rustic room. Even though her mind was screaming at her that this was a terrible idea, that the last place in the house she wanted to be going right then was the creepy room at the top of the steep stairs, her body kept moving without her assistance. In a matter of moments she was standing next to Marsh with her flashlight shining its beam up into the dark.

"You first," Marsh whispered. Chloe swallowed and nodded, not judging him in the least. Had she thought of it, she would have told him to go before he had the chance to use it on her, so fair was fair. As she drew near the bottom step, the wind picked up, whistling under the door behind her, the original front door of the house, now latched tight. Chloe shivered as a draft found her bare legs and traced up her back. Were the old rafters groaning more than normal? Was the very house protesting what she and Marsh were about to do? The rain had not let up, a steady percussive force against the wavy glass in the windows. It was far gloomier now than even it seemed at night. The weight of the storm seemed to press down on her. Chloe felt herself hunching over and had to force her shoulders back as she set foot on the first step.

She could feel Marsh right behind her, his breath on the back of her neck. She paused on the third step, her light wobbling as she got her balance. They both jumped as the window at the top of the stairs came alive with a flash of lightning, followed in close succession by a rolling chorus of thunder that rattled the windows and Chloe's nerve. It didn't help that Marsh let a small shriek escape him. She shot him a glare before continuing on. He was so close now it felt like he was pushing her and she knew it was necessary. If she had been alone she would have turned and run.

By the time they reached the top, the tension was almost too much. Marsh tripped and bumped into her, forcing her up the last step and face-first toward the window.

"Sorry," he whispered. Chloe giggled and realized then that she was having fun. She felt like a character in a book, just like her new favourite, Anne. She knew that this was the type of adventure that the red-haired girl would love and tried to imagine Anne was right there with her.

The rain was much louder in the little room, drumming so hard her ears felt numb. Side by side, they examined the entire empty room. Chloe could see where flat wooden beds had scarred the floor and found a paler spot where perhaps a rug had sat. Aside from that, however, they came up empty.

"Who do you suppose he is?" Marsh asked.

Chloe didn't have an answer. "You tell me, Island boy." It came out harsher than she had meant, so she smiled at him to show she was kidding.

"Well," he spun, light making its way around the bare walls, "he could have been murdered, maybe? His bones buried under the floorboards?"

They both shivered. Chloe was grinning, thinking of her book and the dramatic Anne. "How about an orphan? Somebody made him a slave and worked him so hard he died." Chloe shuddered at the idea, only then remembering she was an orphan now, too. Thankfully she had her Aunt Larry. Neither she nor Anne had to face such a harsh fate.

Marsh was nodding, getting into it. "I know! How about a ship boy lost at sea who swam all the way back to die on the shore." Chloe laughed at Marsh as he pretended to die, falling to the floor.

"Be serious," she said. "How could he swim so far?"

"He came off the Phantom Ship, of course." Marsh shone

the flashlight under his chin, making his face look very spooky.

"What's that?" Chloe asked.

"Big burning schooner," he told her, getting to his feet and dusting himself off. "Been sailing back and forth between us and Nova Scotia for, like, hundreds of years or something."

Chloe snorted, but loved the idea. "Really?"

Marsh was nodding fast. "Really. My Grandpa used to tell us stories about how his dad would take him out to see it when he was a boy. Guess it doesn't happen much anymore. You can look it up, if you want." He was getting defensive. Chloe didn't want to lose the moment.

"Cool, I will."

Marsh immediately relaxed. "I have another idea," he said.

This one hadn't turned out so bad, so Chloe decided to risk it.

"Now what?"

"I think you should talk to him," Marsh said.

Chloe backed up a step. She had kind of been thinking the same thing since the boy had appeared when she spoke to her parents. But she hadn't told Marsh about that. He didn't notice her concern, however, and went on.

"See if you can get him to show, you know? Maybe if you talk to him he'll try to talk back or something."

"Maybe," she said, happy he didn't know her secret after all. "What should I say?"

Marsh shrugged his thin shoulders, light dancing in his hand. "Dunno. Whatever you think he'd like to hear, I guess."

Chloe thought about it for a minute before stepping closer to the window.

"Hi," she said. Her voice cracked. Marsh laughed. She glared at him until he fell silent, one hand over his mouth to hide his smile. "Hi," she tried again. "I live here now. I saw you the other night. You looked sad. I was wondering if I could help you."

Marsh was nodding. "Yeah, that's good. They like help, right?"

Chloe continued. "I don't know if I can," she didn't want to make any promises she couldn't keep, especially to a ghost, "but I'll do my best. But you have to tell me what you want, okay?"

They both waited in the near dark. Chloe could hear the rain easing up, the thunder moving off. Even the sky seemed to be growing lighter. She turned to Marsh.

"I don't think he likes you," she said.

Marsh made a face. "Oh, ha ha, Chloe. Maybe it has to be nighttime?"

"Maybe," she said. She was disappointed. She had hoped he would show up so she could prove to another person that she wasn't crazy. Plus, she did want to help him if she could.

Marsh looked out the window. "Storm's almost over," he said. "I should probably be getting home." He sounded reluctant.

"Okay," Chloe said. "I'll keep you posted, though."

Marsh flashed her a smile. "Great!"

Before either of them had a chance to go down the stairs, Aunt Larry appeared at the bottom. They both jumped and laughed.

"Cookies, if you want them," she said.

"Awesome!" Marsh switched off his light and flew down the stairs after her. Chloe paused, however, waiting. Maybe she had been right. Did the boy not want Marsh to be there? But the moment was over and she knew it. A single shaft of sunlight broke through as the cloud bank passed.

Chloe switched off her own flashlight and followed Marsh to the kitchen.

Chapter Fourteen

The cookies were divine. Chloe had no idea that Aunt Larry could bake. She devoured three before coming up for air and thanking her aunt for them.

Aunt Larry was on her own third by then and winked. "What's going on upstairs?" she asked them.

They shared a guilty look. "Nothing," they said together.

Aunt Larry laughed. "Let me guess. You were either looking for buried treasure or a ghost."

Chloe kept her head down and willed Marsh to shut up. She was relieved, however, when he didn't.

"Totally buried treasure," he was nodding with great enthusiasm. "There has to be some up there, Larry. Maybe a metal detector would find it."

"You're welcome to try," she told him. Chloe pushed the plate of still-warm chocolate chip mounds his way.

He took the hint and stuffed in a whole one. When the phone rang, Aunt Larry went off to find the cordless.

"Promise you won't say anything," Chloe begged.

"Are you kidding?" Marsh said. "Number one, my brothers would make my life way worse if they found out, and number two, they wouldn't believe us anyway. Secret's safe with me." He mimed locking his lips and tossing the key as Aunt Larry returned with the phone in her hand.

"That was your mom," she said to Marsh. "She'd like you home for chores."

Marsh groaned but got up. Aunt Larry snuck him a pair of cookies.

"I don't know that your brothers need to know these exist." She winked.

Marsh hugged her and ran for the door, waving one cookie at Chloe while the other disappeared into his mouth. She shook her head, smiling, as the screen door slammed shut behind him.

Chloe spent the rest of the afternoon helping Aunt Larry clean the house. The familiar activity made her feel much more at home. After a great dinner of stew and homemade bread, Chloe retreated to her room.

She lay awake for a while, trying to decide what to do. Her trusty lamp burned beside her in the dark, keeping her safe. But she wanted to talk to the boy, now more than ever. She reached out and shut off the lamp before retreating under her covers with the picture of her parents and her flashlight, recharged with fresh batteries.

She knew he came when she talked to her mom and dad. But she also wanted to talk to him. So, she decided to include him in her conversation and see what happened.

"We had an amazing storm today," she said to Sophie and Patrick. "Didn't we?" She felt silly talking to the boy, not knowing his name. "It was cool. The sky got so dark and it rained really hard. The thunder was right over the house." The thought of the rain made her think of the accident. "Was there lightning?" she asked her father. "I know it was raining." She hesitated, then went on, speaking to the boy alone. "I was home sick," she spoke above a whisper. "They went out for dinner. I felt rotten. I wanted my mom." Her heart was beating too fast. "When she called to check on me... " Chloe drifted off. She had begged her mom to come home. The babysitter was a stupid teenager who didn't know how to make her feel better.

"Mom said they were coming back early." Chloe felt the tears and the heat in her throat and chest. "I never told anybody." The light wavered in front of her as her eyes filled. "It was my fault," she said. "If I hadn't... if they had stayed at the restaurant like they were supposed to... " The tractor-trailer had skidded on the highway to avoid another accident, jackknifing into her parents' SUV. She had looked up jackknife because no one would tell her what that meant. The photos of trucks bent in half made her shudder. "They would be alive," she admitted out loud for the first time since they had died. "It was all my fault."

She heard the sigh and felt him sit. For a moment, she stayed where she was, not wanting to face him even though he was a ghost. She didn't want to face herself now that she had said it.

At last, she pulled the covers down. The boy was looking at her, the same soft white glow around him. He had short brown hair and dark eyes, though it was almost impossible to tell what colour they were. He didn't seem to have much colour about him at all. She had been right about the suspenders, though, and the buttoned-up white shirt. When she looked back to his face, his expression was so sad it broke her heart. Still, the fear rose up again and she pulled herself away from him, back pressed to the wall, knees drawn up. He reached out to her, as though moving in slow motion. Chloe's hands went to her mouth, fear drowning her sadness. He dropped his hand and bowed his head. Then, he vanished.

Chloe regretted it.

"Don't go!" she called out in a rough whisper. "Come back!"

It was no use. He was gone.

"Fine," she said, climbing out of bed. "I'm sorry. I want you to come back. But if you won't come to me, I'm coming to you."

Determined, Chloe took the flashlight and tiptoed out of her room in pursuit of the ghost boy.

Chapter Fifteen

The second floor hall was empty and very quiet. Chloe made her way with as little noise as possible past Aunt Larry's door to the staircase. She paused to make sure her aunt was still sleeping. The last thing she needed was to have her find Chloe wandering around the house with no explanation why. Aunt Larry was snoring away, however, so Chloe went on.

She didn't use her flashlight until she was downstairs. She hurried to the old part of the house and paused at the bottom of the staircase.

"I'm coming up," she whispered. "Please be there. But don't scare me, okay?" Trusting her message had reached the ghost boy, Chloe climbed to the little room.

Once there, she flashed her light around. It was empty.

"I'm sorry," she said to the still air. "Honest. I... I've never seen a ghost before and it's a little scary. Please come out."

Nothing happened. No glowing boy, not even a flicker.

"I didn't mean to hurt your feelings," Chloe went on. "I really want to help you. But I can't if you won't come back."

Still nothing. Chloe felt her fear fade away. She wasn't sure why, but she wasn't scared of him anymore. To prove it, she switched off her flashlight and stood there in the dark.

"It's okay," she said. "I'm not afraid. You looked so sad. I'm sad, too." She hugged herself. "I miss my mom and dad. It's okay sometimes, like when I'm distracted or doing something new. But then I start to think about it, about them... I worry a lot." She felt safe pouring out her heart to him more than anyone else she knew. "Are they okay where they are? Did they go to heaven like Grammy Sutton said? Do they miss me?" She sighed, the sound reminding her of the boy. "How come you're a ghost and they aren't? I'd give anything to see my mom again. But not if she was sad." Chloe looked out the window toward the garden. "I wish I could change it, go back and make it different. I bet you would, too, or you wouldn't be here."

A soft light caught her attention. Chloe turned and saw the boy standing a few feet away from her. He looked like he was crying.

"I want to help you," she said. "I'm sorry you're sad. Was it horrible?"

He lifted his arm again, holding his hand out to her.

Chloe took a step closer and reached out. When her fingers slid through the edge of him, she shivered. There was nothing there but a bit of a chill.

"Did someone hurt you?" she asked him, knowing he wouldn't answer, but hoping for more clues. "Is that why you're sad?"

In answer, he turned and pointed to the staircase. Chloe followed his gesture and found herself standing on the top step.

"You want me to leave?" She felt hurt. Maybe he didn't want her help after all.

He continued to point. Chloe tried to follow where he was pointing and realized he wasn't showing her the stairs, but the low wall above them. It was so low she almost had to duck every time she came up.

She pointed at it. "Is that what you want me to look at?"

The boy vanished. Chloe was startled and disoriented. His glow had given her some light. Curious, she switched on her flashlight and shone it on the overhang. It was plain wood, like the rest of the upstairs, rough in places with bits of old bark curling away. She examined it, leaning forward to touch it. She felt each board, one at a time, all the way to the corner. She struggled to reach and had to go down one step to do so. When she did, she felt the last board move under her hand. Excited, Chloe slid it aside. There was a hole behind it. She shone her flashlight in but was too short to see very far.

Trying to be brave, Chloe stuck her hand inside and

met cobwebs. She pulled back with a little shriek before trying again. This time, she found something with the edges of her fingertips. She tugged at the hard, flat thing with the tips of her nails and felt it slide closer to her. After some coaxing, she was able to get it close enough to get her fingers around it and pull it out.

It was a book. Chloe held it up under her light. The cover was dusty and very worn, made of brown cloth, from what she could tell, cracked and bent at the edges. It was covered in a layer of dust and cobwebs. She blew on it to clear the clinging stuff away. Eager to have a look inside, she started down the stairs. She paused, though, and went back up long enough to whisper "thank you" into the room before retreating back to her own.

She was much less careful on her return trip, but made it without waking Aunt Larry anyway. She found an old sock and dusted the book clean. She climbed into bed with it and took it with her into her tent. Fingers trembling with excitement, she opened the cover.

The paper was thin and brittle, little bits of the edges breaking off in her fingers. It was yellowed with age and looked like it might have gotten wet at some point, drying with wavy light-brown borders around the pages. Inside the front cover was a sketch of a small house, faded but still visible. On the facing page she read:

The Private Journal of J.

Chloe ran her fingertips over the words. "Hi, J," she

said. She flipped the page. It clung to the next one by the corner. It took her a couple of soft tugs to get them apart. The first page was dated December 25, 1941.

My Christmas present is perfect! Momma knew what I wanted. I shall keep all of my thoughts and feelings in this book and share them with no one until I am a famous author someday.

Chloe smiled. He sounded kind of like Marsh.

December 26, 1941

J is jealous and tried to take my journal. He wants to read it. He seems to think that just because he is my twin brother I should share everything with him, but I disagree. To my relief, so does Momma. I have decided to secret this journal in the oldest part of the house, safe from prying eyes. If you are reading this and you are not me, please put this journal back.

Chloe felt slightly guilty for ignoring J's request, like a bit of a snoop. Still, she turned the page, eager to go on, but the paper was stuck again. Not wanting to tear it, she closed it instead. Her eyes were getting heavy anyway and she wanted to be able to read it all the way through.

He wouldn't have shown me where it was if he didn't want me to read it, she told herself in an effort to ease the pang of guilt.

Chloe kissed her parents' photo good night and placed it between the first two pages of the book before tucking the whole thing under her pillow. As she switched off her flashlight and set it aside, she whispered into the quiet of her room.

"Good night, J," she said. "Thanks for the book. I promise I'll read it all and find out what happened so I can help you." It felt very important for her to do it.

For the first time since she had arrived, Chloe fell into a deep and peaceful sleep.

Chapter Sixteen

Chloe was halfway through breakfast before Aunt Larry brought it up.

"What were you doing out and around so late last night?" Her aunt was sipping her cup of coffee and looking right at her. Chloe's heart stopped. She hadn't been as careful as she thought.

"Nothing," she said, focusing her attention on her toast and peanut butter.

"I don't like you wandering around the house in the middle of the night," Aunt Larry said. "You could fall down the stairs and hurt yourself."

"I'm okay," Chloe said. "Honest. I just... " She hated lying to her aunt but couldn't tell her the truth. "I was going to the bathroom and thought I heard something downstairs."

"Even worse," Aunt Larry said, but she was smiling. "You're braver than you should be. Braver than I am." She chuckled. "Next time, come get me, okay?"

Chloe filled her mouth with toast so she wouldn't have to say anything else. Her deception seemed to have worked because her aunt changed the subject.

"We've been invited to the MacKenzies'," she said. "Sunday is big meal day here. Mary thought you'd like to taste a real Island chicken dinner."

Chloe almost choked on her breakfast. Chicken! She struggled to swallow as the cute little chickens from Marsh's yard pranced through her memory. Larry was laughing at her.

"Don't worry," she said, understanding Chloe's reluctance. "Nobody you know."

Chloe giggled. "Good," she said.

"I don't know if I'll be able to take you with me to Africa after all." Her aunt winked at her. "You might not like the food."

Chloe didn't want to think about it. "How can you stand it?" she asked.

Aunt Larry pretended to shudder. "You have no idea," she said. "The first time I went, they asked me to help make dinner. That involved killing a small pig." She rolled her eyes. "There was no way. I could barely eat for a week. I didn't know what a huge honour it was. They were having a feast for me. They got by on very little. I almost insulted them when I couldn't eat it. I was lucky, though. My guide had seen it before." She was smiling at the memory. "You get used to it when you're hungry enough."

Chloe was quite certain she would never in her life be that hungry, ever.

"So we'll leave here around 12:30, okay?"

Chloe was confused. "I thought you said dinner."

"Oh yes, right," Aunt Larry said on her way to her office with a fresh cup of coffee. "Another Island thing. Dinner is lunch and supper is dinner. Funny, huh?"

Chloe agreed. It didn't stop her from worrying about the whole thing, however. She fretted all morning about seeing Marsh's brothers again, not wanting to relive the embarrassment of two days before. Plus, she wanted time to fix the journal so she could read it. She was able to get a few more pages separated by the time Aunt Larry called for her, but not many. It was a slow and frustrating process and Chloe was sure her aunt could help her. But getting help with the journal would lead to telling Aunt Larry too much and Chloe didn't want to share.

Aunt Larry was standing by the edge of the field when Chloe came down. She was disappointed.

"We aren't driving?" she asked, thinking about the last time she walked to Marsh's and how hot and dirty she was when she got there.

Aunt Larry smiled at her. "The fresh air is good for us," she said.

Under her breath Chloe muttered something unhappy about fresh air, but followed anyway.

Instead of cutting through the field like Marsh had, however, Aunt Larry walked along the edge for a bit before turning in. Chloe was delighted, then angry.

"A path?" She stopped at the head of it so Aunt Larry had to pause and turn to see her. "He dragged me all the way through that," she pointed at the long, heavy grass, "when there was a path?" She was going to hit Marsh when she saw him.

Aunt Larry was laughing. "Come on, you," she said. "We're going to be late."

When they emerged in the MacKenzies' yard, they were greeted with great gusto by the very enthusiastic Shep. His baying barks brought Marsh running. He was scrubbed pink, his curls smashed into some kind of order behind his ears which, Chloe noticed, stuck out a little.

"Dinner's ready!" he said before turning and running back toward the house. He looked over his shoulder once and waved for them to hurry. "C'mon! You'll miss the crunchy stuffing!"

Not sure what to expect, Chloe picked up the pace. By the time she and Aunt Larry reached the front door, Marsh had already gone inside. His mother, Mary, met them with a beaming smile. She had deep red hair and soft blue eyes. Her pale yellow sundress was protected by a red and white checkered apron. She hugged Aunt Larry before turning to Chloe.

"It's very nice to meet you," Mary said. Chloe smiled back, shyness returning.

They were ushered through the small porch full of rubber boots and plastic tubs and boxes of old nails and bits of odds and ends, and into the main room with a big wood stove in the corner. Chloe followed Aunt Larry to the dining room. The whole house smelled great. Chloe's mouth watered as she sat down between Rebecca and her aunt. Marsh sat across from her. Chloe smiled at Rebecca who smiled back and squeezed her hand.

"Nice to see you, Chloe," Rebecca said.

The rest of the kids offered their noisy hellos that turned to pandemonium. Chloe was overwhelmed by them. They shouted and yelled back and forth at each other while Bill, Marsh's father, stood at the head of the table carving a golden chicken. Marsh and his brothers kept taking turns stealing from a big white bowl of what looked like bread. Sophie had never cooked stuff like this.

Marsh leaned forward after a nab and tossed some onto Chloe's plate. It was bread with some green herb in it. It was roasted brown on the outside and looked soft on the inside. She popped it into her mouth and was surprised by the crunch. It was delicious, full of chicken flavour and butter and bread and the herb that was on it.

"Good, yeah?" Marsh was munching on his own.

Chloe nodded, eyes wide. Mary was smiling.

"Larry said you had never had roast chicken dinner before," she said. "It's a favourite. I hope you like it."

Chloe did. Mashed potatoes were piled high on her

plate, to be smothered by hot golden gravy. Buttered carrots and caramelized sweet potatoes joined them. Aunt Larry gave her a generous slice of chicken breast from the serving plate, one with the skin still on. Then she added a dollop of some kind of deep purple jelly.

"Blackberry," she told Chloe. "We'll make some this fall. You'll love it."

It was all topped off with hot, homemade biscuits and real butter. Chloe waited with the others, as impatient as the boys, while little Grace said, fittingly enough, grace. Then, she dug in. She was grinning at Marsh as much as he was smiling at her. The food was delicious and she didn't stop shovelling until her plate was empty.

Mary's eyes were bright when she asked if it was okay. Chloe almost choked and had to take a drink while she nodded with great enthusiasm. Aunt Larry laughed beside her, but was eating with as much enjoyment.

It wasn't long before everyone sat back with happy groans of too-full stomachs. Even the twins, who seemed to be bottomless pits and had fought over thirds, were satisfied.

Bill leaned over and kissed Mary on the cheek. "That was delicious, dear," he said. The chorus agreed, Chloe among them.

"I hope we left room for dessert." Mary winked at Chloe. She wasn't quite as full as she thought she was.

"So, Chloe," Bill said, "I hear you had a close encounter with the grain pile the other day."

Chloe blushed. Mary cuffed her husband on the arm.

"Leave her, Bill," she said, looking at Chloe with sympathy. "It wasn't her fault the boys dragged her into that."

Bill's eyes were twinkling. He had pale red hair and a ton of freckles like his kids. "Did it take long to get all the chaff out of your hair?"

"No, Mr. MacKenzie," Chloe said. That made him laugh.

"Good for you, kiddo," he answered. "At least you had a helping hand, right Marshall?"

It was Marsh's turn to blush.

"I think we could find something else to talk about," Mary said. "Larry told me you're reading Anne of Green Gables." The boys all groaned, but Rebecca was smiling at her mother.

"Yes, Mrs. MacKenzie," Chloe said.

"It was my favourite book when I was your age," Mary said with a smile, getting up and gathering a few dishes. "I loved how brave she was and how she was always getting herself into and out of trouble. It helped that we have the same colour hair."

"And the same temper," Bill grinned, dodging Mary's elbow as she loaded up with plates.

Chloe wasn't sure what to make of the MacKenzies with their huge family and the way they teased each other. Sure, Patrick had been great to joke about, but both he and her mom were quiet people, nothing like the loud, enthusiastic clan she found herself surrounded by. Still, Mary's comments about Anne hit close to home. Who would have thought I'd be having my own adventure?

Rebecca got up to help but when Aunt Larry and Chloe

did the same, Mary waved them off. "Guests sit," she said before disappearing into the kitchen.

Bill was still grinning. Chloe's dad had been a tease as well. Patrick loved nothing more than to get a rise out of her or Sophie, whoever would take the bait. Because of that, Chloe wasn't offended when Bill went on. He was very nice and his smile was good-natured.

"How are you liking the old homestead, Chloe?"

"It's okay," she said. "I like it."

"She had a bit of an encounter with Joseph her first day," Aunt Larry said.

Chloe blushed again. She didn't want to think about it.

Mary had returned, however, and was looking at her with sympathy. "Was he horrible?" she asked.

Chloe shrugged, wishing Aunt Larry had kept it to herself.

"He's not so bad," Bill said. "He had a hard life. But it's best if you just keep off his property if you can."

"Makes a bad name for the family," Mary said before leaving again. Bill looked sad, however. Then, the mischief came back. He leaned toward Chloe and motioned for her to come closer, which she did.

"Seen any ghosts yet?"

She was so startled she stared at him. Meanwhile, Mary returned for more dishes and this time smacked him across the back of the head.

"Bill! Don't you fill that child's head with stuff like that!" Her smile was an apology. "Don't pay any attention to him, sweetie," she said. "There aren't any ghosts in the house." She made a mad face at him before leaving with her third load.

Bill ignored her and leaned closer. "Is too," he said. "My brothers and I saw one, once, when we were your age." His eyes sparkled with mischief. "We used to dare each other to spend the night there, but no one would. Then, one night, we're standing outside, right? In the yard below that little window in the old part of the house, you know, where Larry has that deck now?"

She knew the window, all right.

"So, there we were," Bill's voice got louder as all the kids stopped to listen, "fighting over who was going to stay and who wasn't, when my brother Bobby lets out this horrible scream." Everyone was staring at him, eyes wide. Mary came back from the kitchen. This time she sighed as he went on. "We all look over at Bobby and he's pointing up at the window. I was scared but I looked up, too."

"And?" Even Liam was caught up in it, and he was sixteen.

"There was a face in the window," Bill said, voice quiet so they all had to lean in to hear. "A boy's face. It was staring. Right. At. Us." As he spoke, he pointed at each of the kids, punctuating his words. Little Grace cuddled to Rebecca who sat down again.

"What did you do?" the twins asked together, eyes huge.

"We ran, of course," Bill said, sitting up, voice back to normal. "Ran screaming like rabbits. Scared the bejesus out of me."

Chloe tried to fake amazement while Mary sliced a big chocolate cake.

"Cool," she said. "I'll be sure to watch for him."

Bill looked at her, clearly shocked. Mary, however, laughed and handed Chloe a very large piece of cake. Then Bill laughed, too, and winked at her.

"Any idea who he might be?" Chloe asked.

Bill shook his head. "It's just a story, Chloe," he told her.

She exchanged a look with Marsh. Maybe over the years his dad had managed to convince himself it was "just a story," but they knew the story was true.

Chapter Seventeen

Marsh cornered Chloe in the yard.

"I swear I didn't say anything to him," he told her in a whisper, breathless with the effort to get the words out.

"I know," Chloe said. "Funny, though, isn't it? I wonder how many other people saw him but won't believe it."

"Did you see him again?" Marsh asked.

"Last night," Chloe said. She was about to tell him about the diary when she hesitated. She wanted to keep it to herself. The feeling went away, however. Chloe told him everything that had happened.

Marsh was jumping up and down with excitement by the time she finished. "He didn't say anything?"

"No. But I'm reading the journal. It's kind of hard, though. It's damaged and I don't want to wreck it."

"This is the best summer ever!" He hugged her before she knew he was going to, bumping her nose against his collarbone so hard it stung for a moment. "I'm so glad you're here! I was sure this was going to be just another boring break, but this is awesome!" His face fell as he realized what he was saying. "I didn't mean... sorry, Chloe."

She was used to him by now and didn't hold it against him. "It's okay. I know what you meant."

In typical Marsh fashion, he forgot all about it.

"Can I see it?" He started pulling on her arm. "Let's go!"

Chloe held back, that same odd surge of desire to keep it private making her resist. She didn't really have a reason for it. But the boy wanted her to have it. He hadn't shown up for Marsh, after all, only her. But she knew Marsh might be able to help her figure out how to get more pages apart, so she went with him.

She waved at Aunt Larry in passing. "See you at home," her aunt called after her. Marsh was already on his way to the field. Chloe found the path and followed.

She felt her excitement rising as they pounded their way through the house and to her room. She slipped the book out from under her pillow and held it up so Marsh could see. As she did, her parents' photo slid from between the pages and fluttered to the floor. Chloe felt her face turning red as Marsh bent and picked it up. She wanted more than anything to snatch it back from him, but held herself still as he looked at it.

"They seem nice," he said, handing it to her after a moment.

"Thanks," she said. She tucked it back under her pillow, embarrassed that Marsh now knew part of her secret, but when she looked into his eyes he was smiling, which made her feel much better.

"Let's have a look," he said.

Chloe deposited the book in his eager hands. She was about to caution him to be careful of it, now fully aware of Marsh's gung-ho nature, but didn't have to. He used the tip of his finger to open the cover by one corner. He squinted at the picture and the handwriting.

"J. Who is J?" He flipped another page and winced as the paper crumbled. "It's really old, huh?"

"1941," Chloe said, pointing at the date.

"Maybe there's more stuff where you found it!" He handed the book back to her.

The thought had crossed her mind but she hadn't had a chance to check. She returned the journal to its hiding place under her pillow before following Marsh to the other end of the house.

He was taller than her so he was able to reach farther into the cubbyhole above the old stairs. Aside from the stub of a pencil, however, it was empty. Chloe slipped the pencil in her pocket with plans to keep it with the book. Marsh, excited by the find, did another thorough search of the room but came up empty. By the time they had finished, they were both disappointed.

"I'll keep at it," Chloe told him. "Find out who he was

and what happened. Maybe the journal will have more clues."

"He wanted you to have it for a reason," Marsh agreed. "But one thing is sure. He lived here and that narrows down the possibilities." His eyes lit up. "I know where we might be able to find him, too!"

"Where?" Chloe asked.

"The family graveyard!" He smacked his forehead with the palm of his hand. "Why didn't I think of it before?"

Chloe didn't like the sound of it. She had bad memories of the last graveyard she had been in. "Where is it?"

Marsh shuddered with a mix of fear and excitement. "That's the only problem," he said. "It's on the other side of the fence, behind Joseph's cottage."

Chloe hesitated. She did not want to have another confrontation with that mean old man. The memory of him yelling at her was still fresh. But, the ghost boy needed her, didn't he?

"A lot of families had their own plots in the old days," Marsh told her. "They're all over the Island. I'm not sure when they stopped using them, but maybe he's there. If not, we could always check the church down the road. That's where Gramps is buried."

"Should we check there first?" She was nervous about risking it.

"The other one is closer," he said. "Don't worry. Joseph is pretty harmless. And we'll go at night, after dark so he doesn't see us. He won't even know we were there. I know how to get to the house without being seen."

"How?" Chloe asked.

He blushed, the red filling in his freckles. "Liam and the twins and I... we sometimes go over there at Halloween and, you know... trick."

"No wonder he's so cranky," Chloe said. "You guys are mean."

"No way!" Marsh defended himself. "He's been that way forever, honest! Even my dad says so."

They both jumped at the sound of the front door banging shut. Chloe heard Aunt Larry calling her name. They scrambled down the stairs and into the main part of the house before she could catch them upstairs.

"I'll see you at eleven o'clock," he whispered to her before dashing with a wave past Aunt Larry and out the door.

Chapter Eighteen

Chloe was so nervous that night she couldn't eat dinner. Aunt Larry, it turned out, wasn't hungry either, blaming it on the huge lunch they'd had, so Chloe was off the hook. She said an early good night to her aunt and retreated to her room and the book.

Chloe set the pencil on her vanity and went to work on the pages of the journal. She was about to give up when the last bit of resistance let go and all the sheets were free.

Eager to find out more, Chloe started to read.

December 27, 1941

M only wants to talk about Angus Morrison all the time. She keeps telling Momma she is in love with him and will die if he goes off to France with the other boys. I think she is being selfish. Those boys are fighting for our country against the evil Nazis. Everyone knows that. Even the Americans are getting in on it, now. I wish I was old enough to go too. I would kill more Nazis than anyone else.

December 29, 1941

J is mad at me again. It snowed so much the last few days that everything is covered in white. Poppa had a hard time getting the front door open after the storm. J didn't want to help even though we had to get a way cleared so we could feed the cows. When I told him so, he told me to shut up and Momma got mad at him. Now he is being punished and he says it is my fault. My teacher, Miss T, told me that twins are supposed to be really close and the very best of friends. Why aren't J and I?

Chloe continued to read. As time passed, J wrote less often, but there was at least one entry every week. She was fascinated by his life, living on the farm, helping his parents. They didn't have electricity yet, being so far from the road.

March 17, 1941

Momma was complaining today to Poppa about how he still hasn't completed the finishing work on the new part of the house. It is an old argument. Poppa's insisted on finishing the widow cottage for Grammy first before he does anything else for Momma. That makes her blood boil since she thinks Poppa put his own mother ahead of all of us. And now that the war is on, it's harder to get some things. Poppa told me this morning he is going to show me how to make nails out of old horseshoes.

I still like the old part of the house better. I like to write up here. It makes me feel like Gramps is still alive and remember that Poppa used to be young, like me.

Chloe had been feeling a connection between herself and J; it became stronger with every entry she read. By the time May rolled around in the diary, she felt like he was an old friend.

May 11, 1941

I had to stay home from school today and help Poppa with the fields. I didn't want to but we all have to help out. Miss T says I am her best student and wants me to keep studying over the summer break. I would love to. She even thinks that I should go to university someday and maybe be a teacher or a doctor or something. It makes me happy to think that I could. I know Poppa would be disappointed if I didn't farm like him but I love school!

Chloe found herself smiling. She liked school a lot, too. They had so much in common! For a time, reading his journal, she forgot that he was not only a ghost, but that he had lived seventy years ago, long before she was born.

May 12, 1941

J found this and showed it to Poppa. I am so angry! He didn't have the right! Poppa said it was okay and punished J for taking my journal but now I feel terrible that he knows I don't want to be a farmer. I have a new hiding place for it that J will never find. I wish he would just leave me alone!

Chloe did, too. How dare he? She read on through the diary. It soon became apparent that the mean J (as she had begun to think of him) did his best to make her J look or feel bad. Chloe found herself hating the other twin and commiserating with her friend over the bullying.

At last, Chloe came to July 14, 1941.

J tried to accuse me of stealing his yo-yo. Like I care about his stupid toy! He yelled at me and pushed me down in the yard. Poppa caught him, but J wouldn't stop. He told Poppa I stole it but I didn't. Poppa was mad at me! He thinks I'm lying when it's J that's lying! It's not fair! If I do find his stupid yo-yo, I'll throw it in the ocean and he'll never see it again, ever!

There were several round watermarks on the page that had nothing to do with the other damage. Chloe realized they were left behind by his tears. She touched each of them with her fingertips before turning the page. There was nothing to see. The remaining pages, what few were left, were empty.

Chloe sat back, disappointed. She wanted more! And there was no clue here as to what had happened to J. She knew he must have died right after. With a start she looked at her calendar. It was July 12, two days before the entry. She shivered. She was reading his journal seventy years almost to the day of his death.

Frustrated, Chloe closed the book. As she did, she noticed the red numbers on her clock turn over to 10:30. Determined now to see it through, she put the book away and got ready to meet Marsh.

Chapter Nineteen

Chloe made sure she was extra quiet on her way out that night. She didn't want Aunt Larry asking any more questions. Instead of waiting inside, she went ahead and snuck out the back door and onto the deck. The night was clear and warm like a hug. There was a light breeze, enough to ruffle her hair and make the trees whisper, but that was all. She sat in the dark and waited, lost in 1941.

Right at eleven o'clock, Marsh appeared around the back of the house. He was dressed all in black. Chloe tried not to laugh. He was acting weird, like he thought he was a spy or something. She stifled her giggle behind her hand as he crept up to her, looking this way and that as if he had been followed.

She got up and went to him while he continued to scope out the backyard.

"Ready?" she asked.

"Shhh!" he hissed at her. "No talking until we're a safe distance. Never know who could be watching." He slunk off into the night. Chloe, still amused, started after him. A flicker of light above her brought her to a halt. The boy was standing in the window, watching her. Chloe waved at him. He vanished.

Knowing she was doing what he wanted made her feel better. Chloe turned and plodded after Marsh. She caught up with him at the edge of the grass where he waited for her with obvious impatience. He moved off again, leaving her to follow. She had to hurry, knowing how fast Marsh moved, but needn't have worried. He was so wrapped up in his game that he was going much more slowly, stopping to check imagined noises and make sure they hadn't been followed. Chloe found it hilarious.

Once they were far enough away from the house, Marsh spoke up.

"Can't be too careful," he told her. "Spies everywhere. Need to keep this operation clean and professional."

Chloe nodded in agreement. "Gotcha," she said. "Now what?"

"We head for the back of Joseph's place," he said. "After I make sure the coast is clear."

A thought occurred to her as they slunk through the night (him by choice, her because he would shoot looks at her if she didn't).

"Why didn't we ask your parents?" She felt kind of

foolish as she realized how much easier it would have been. It was seventy years ago. They would know who the boy was.

Marsh shrugged, dropping out of character for a minute.

"More fun this way," he said. "Besides, I've seen the stones. I know what we're looking for. Follow me." He went back to slinking.

Chloe was trying to decide if Island kids were more weird than cool. Her friends in Ottawa would never do anything like what she and Marsh were up to.

Chloe could see the fence up ahead in the glow coming from the cottage windows. Just on their side of it, Marsh grabbed her and hauled her into the grass where he crouched, watching Joseph's place with an eagle eye.

"Have to wait for the lights to go out," he said. Chloe found a comfortable spot and sat down. It wasn't long before the leftover moisture in the grass wet through the seat of her jeans. And the mosquitoes were out. After a few minutes of slapping, Chloe was losing her enthusiasm for the whole adventure. Marsh, however, had thought of bugs and produced a small can of spray. After a liberal dose of the stuff, Chloe was no longer tormented by insects, but she was stinky. That coupled with her wet jeans made her wish she could just go home, but she decided to stay. J was worth it.

When Marsh produced a large chocolate bar from his jacket and gave her half, Chloe started warming back up to the idea. Especially when her stomach growled to remind her she had skipped dinner.

It seemed like forever that they sat there in the long, damp grass. Marsh kept lighting up his watch from one of the buttons on the side. Chloe tried not to focus on the time. Every time he turned it on, however, she couldn't help herself. 11:12. 11:17. 11:25. The time dragged on and on. And her candy bar was a long-forgotten memory. She amused herself by wadding up bits of grass and mud and throwing them at Marsh. Every time she hit him, he would shoot her a look that made her want to laugh out loud. His attempts to shush her led to another packed ball tossed his way.

As his watch read 11:43, the light in the cottage went dark. Marsh made her wait another five minutes before parting the barbed wire and helping her through the fence. On the other side, she was surprised to find Marsh was starting to rub off on her. She felt like a secret agent or a treasure hunter in dangerous territory and decided it was cool after all.

Halfway to the cottage, they startled some birds nesting in the grass and had to hunch down, hearts pounding, to wait and see if the old man noticed. Chloe tried hard not to giggle but a few snorts escaped her. Marsh was grinning, his teeth shining in the faint light of the rising moon. The cottage remained dark and silent. After a bit of a wait they moved on.

Chloe's sense of adventure followed her all the way to the tiny yard. They circled around away from the rusted old car and the small garden that faced Aunt Larry's house. Marsh led her with complete confidence, again in silence, through the long grass toward the back of the property.

The backyard was full of old metal parts and machinery. Chloe was distracted by the sight, but when she drifted closer for a look, she found herself being pulled back on course by Marsh. Beyond that different kind of graveyard, they stumbled out of the tangle of long grass and into a small patch of tidiness. Chloe could just make out the stones in the darkness. She shivered next to Marsh as he eased open the small iron gate that was the only entry. The cemetery was surrounded by a short fence and was neat and tidy, unlike the rest of the property. Chloe eased through the open gate and cringed away from the very tall stone that leaned with age over the entry. She followed Marsh inside, being careful to shield her flashlight with her hand so that only the stones were illuminated.

After a few moments searching, she heard Marsh hiss at her. Chloe went to him and looked at the headstone he was lighting up with his own flashlight. Her heart skipped a beat as she read the stone.

April 13, 1931 – July 14, 1941
Joshua Robert MacKenzie
Gone Too Soon
But Never Forgotten

Chloe felt tears well in her eyes. She reached out and

touched the stone.

"He was our age," Marsh said, doing the math.

Chloe knew that but didn't know how.

"Joshua," she said.

He appeared behind the stone in a glow of light. Marsh let out a yell and fell back, losing his flashlight in the grass. Chloe caught her breath, but wasn't afraid. Joshua's face was covered in tears as he looked down at his own grave, then back to her before vanishing.

She registered Marsh beside her as she pulled out a small notebook and jotted down the dates on the stone. Marsh suddenly started pulling on her arm, his flashlight now dead in his hand. She was aware then of the light behind her and turned to see the interior of the cottage lit up. She heard the screen door bang open and saw Joseph emerge. He had a shotgun.

"Who's out there?" he roared into the night. Marsh pulled Chloe along to the gate and out into the long grass, staying as low as possible. Joseph was waving the gun around and shouting. "Show yourselves, you little varmints!"

Marsh wormed deeper into the grass and watched the old man. He flashed a grin at Chloe who found she wasn't scared at all. She grinned back, feeling exhilarated, her mind going to Anne and the redhead's bravery. Maybe some of what she had read of her fellow orphan had rubbed off.

Chloe and Marsh sat there for a long time, listening to Joseph yelling at them but knowing they were safe.

The old man gave up and went back inside. Chloe could no longer hold in her giggles. She and Marsh laughed and laughed, as quietly as possible. Chloe clutched at her ribs as they started to ache, wiping at tears that squeezed from her eyes. Marsh was grunting little snorts of laughter, and kept slapping the ground with his hand.

When their adrenaline-fed humour ran out, Marsh led Chloe back to the fence and helped her through it. Safe on the other side, Marsh was enthusiastic.

"That was awesome!" He jumped up and down, fists pumping the air. "Not only did we pull one over on the old crank, I got to see a ghost!" He high-fived Chloe. "You're the best thing that ever happened to me," he told her.

Chloe laughed at him. "Thanks," she said. "You're not so bad yourself."

They parted ways at the grass border of her backyard.

"We'll do some research tomorrow and see what we can find out about him," Marsh said. "I'll be over in the morning, okay? Wait for me!" He trotted off into the night, waving at her.

Chloe waited until she couldn't see him anymore before sneaking back into the house.

Chapter Twenty

Chloe sagged against her bedroom door. She had made it back to her room without alerting Aunt Larry. She was concerned about the smell of her clothes and hair from the bug spray, but knew she couldn't risk a shower that late at night without waking her aunt.

Instead, she went right to her desk and the journal.

"I found you," she said. "Joshua. I know who you are now. I'm so glad I went. Marsh was right." She giggled. "We could have found out somehow, but this was way more fun." She sat back in her chair. "Now we just have to figure out what we can do to help you move on."

Chloe turned at the glimmer of light. Joshua was standing by her door. He gestured toward it before floating right through it. Chloe was speechless. He wanted her to follow him, that much was obvious. She went to her door and peeked out. Joshua was at the bottom of the stairs. He pointed toward the interior of the house.

Unable to resist, she followed. She was almost to the stairs when the bathroom door opened and Aunt Larry stepped out. She shrieked at the sight of Chloe standing there. Chloe glanced down the staircase and saw Joshua disappear.

"Chloe!" Aunt Larry let out a big breath. "You scared the daylights out of me."

Chloe muttered an apology. She knew how she looked, fully dressed, jeans still wet and stinking of bug spray. She saw her aunt taking it all in and witnessed the astonishment turn to concern.

"Where have you been?" Aunt Larry switched on the hall light to get a better look. Chloe was torn between being embarrassed and wanting to follow Joshua.

"Nowhere," she lied, knowing it was obvious she was lying but unable to come up with anything else right then.

For the first time ever, Chloe saw Aunt Larry get mad.

"Chloe Olivia Sutton," her aunt said, using the dreaded three names while crossing her arms over her chest and scowling, "I want to know where you were and what you were doing. It's after midnight!" Larry threw her hands up in the air.

"I was outside in the garden," Chloe mumbled.

"Alone?" Aunt Larry stressed the word.

"Yes," Chloe said.

"I see. And why were you in the garden?"

"Um… " Chloe couldn't think of an excuse. "Because."

"So you weren't with Marsh doing something you shouldn't be doing?" Aunt Larry was still mad, but the edge of anger had left her voice. Still, Chloe didn't want to get her friend in trouble.

"No," she said.

"Since there isn't a can of bug spray to be found in this house," her aunt said, "I'm going to assume you're still lying to me. Chloe, just tell me." Larry took a step toward her. "It's okay, really. I'm not mad. I… I want you to be safe and that cliff can be dangerous this time of night. Tell me you didn't go to the beach."

Chloe shook her head, miserable. She didn't want to worry her aunt, but she wasn't going to tell her the truth, either.

"Do I have to call the MacKenzies?"

Chloe looked up at her, horrified. "No!" This was all Marsh's fault, the whole stupid graveyard thing, but she still wanted to keep him out of it. After all, she had no idea how much he would spill if confronted.

"Then tell me." Aunt Larry was in a no-nonsense mood, but Chloe couldn't.

"No," she said.

Her aunt looked startled. "Chloe!" Larry took a deep breath before saying anything else. "You answer me when I ask you a question, young lady."

Chloe shook her head. "No," she said.

Larry was flabbergasted. "I am not ready for this," she said in a low voice, to herself, before speaking to Chloe again. "Fine. Go to your room. We'll talk in the morning."

Chloe almost rebelled. She needed to find out what Joshua wanted! But the look on Aunt Larry's face turned her around and sent her marching to her room. Chloe closed and locked her door and ran to her bed, tears rising in her eyes. She felt terrible lying to Aunt Larry. Sophie would be so ashamed of her. But she couldn't share the story of the ghost boy. It was hers. Aunt Larry would find some way to stop her from helping Joshua, she knew it. She imagined telling a therapist that there was a ghost in her house who wanted her to help him. She'd be off to the mental ward before she could turn around.

As she bundled her smelly self under the covers, Chloe admitted there was another more private and resounding reason. As long as she focused on Joshua, she didn't think about her parents quite so much and the hurt of losing them was less.

Chapter Twenty-One

Chloe managed to avoid Aunt Larry the next morning, rising late for a thorough shower before helping herself to some cereal that she took with her into the living room. She could hear her aunt moving around from kitchen to office, but kept her head down over her computer so she wouldn't have to confront her. The longer she went without talking to her aunt, the worse she felt about the whole thing, but it was still easier not to. Instead, Chloe did her best to be patient as the Internet search engine ground out answers to her questions.

An hour older but no wiser, Chloe snapped the lid shut. Dial-up was going to be the end of her social life, she knew it, not to mention making it impossible for her to research anything. Bummed, she headed for the kitchen in time to see Marsh raising his hand to knock.

One look at his beaming face made her cringe inside. She was not in the sharing mood. Her friendship with Joshua had become so personal that the last thing she wanted was to have Marsh bumbling about in it, ruining everything. Chloe paused, frozen by indecision. Marsh was bouncing on the other side of the door, watching her with those sad-puppy eyes. Try as she might, Chloe couldn't say no.

"Hi, Marsh," she said as she opened the door. He bounded inside.

"Ready?"

"For what?" Chloe was feeling cranky and out of sorts, not the best mood to be dealing with Marsh.

"Research!" He didn't seem to notice.

"I tried," she complained. She hated the whine in her own voice but couldn't help it. "Stupid dial-up takes forever."

Marsh nodded in sympathy. "Yeah, I know," he said. "High-speed any day now. But that's not what I mean. Mom's going to town and she said we could come."

"And that helps us how?" Chloe wasn't in the mood to be cheered up. She slumped on a stool with her arms crossed over her chest.

"We'll go to the archives," he said.

"What's that?" she asked

"Kind of like a library, except they have old stuff," he told her.

"Great, Marsh," Chloe answered with some bitterness. "Just the place I want to go in the summer." She scowled out the kitchen door at the sun. Stupid nice day, she thought.

He remained undaunted. “Last year my class went to the archives in Charlottetown. We had to do historical research for a particular day of a particular year. Our teacher gave us assignments.”

“So?” Chloe demanded.

“They showed us how to use microfiche,” he said.

“We’re going fishing?” Chloe knew she was being mean but didn’t care.

Marsh made a face at her. “No, silly. Microfiche. It’s a little film roll they use to store old newspapers.”

Chloe perked at that. He was getting somewhere.

“So you think if we go and look at the newspapers we can find out what happened to Joshua?” When she said it she felt better. This was progress!

Marsh, meanwhile, was nodding so hard she thought his freckles might pop off. “And if we can narrow down the date using the diary and the tombstone, we can figure out where to look.”

Chloe hopped down from the stool. “July 14, 1941,” she said. “That was the date of the last entry and the date he died.”

“Then we look from July 14 to July 16 or so and we find it,” he said. “Easy as pie.”

“When do we go?” Chloe’s excitement ebbed as soon as the words were out of her mouth. She wasn’t even sure she could go after the whole scene with Aunt Larry. Marsh must have seen her expression change.

"What's wrong?" he asked.

"I saw him again last night," she admitted in a whisper. "After I snuck back in. I tried to follow him but Aunt Larry caught me. She knew we'd been out. I had to lie to her. Don't worry," she told him as his face fell, "I told her I was alone."

Marsh thought about it for a moment then shrugged. "What's the worst that can happen?"

"I'd have to stay home," Chloe said.

"But I could look for us," he said. "Besides, if she was that mad, my mom would have heard about it by now."

Chloe admitted that was true. Biting the bullet and with Marsh close behind her, she knocked on Aunt Larry's office door. She and Marsh both peeked their heads in when Larry called for them to enter.

"Hi, Larry," Marsh said.

Aunt Larry leaned back from her computer and smiled at him.

"What are you two up to today?" Her eyes fixed on Chloe. She wasn't grounded after all.

"Mom and I are going to town," he told her. "Can Chloe come?"

"Sure," Larry said. "Will you be back for lunch?"

"Probably," he said. "She has errands."

"Have fun," she waved at them as she turned back to her monitor. Marsh poked Chloe and grinned before dashing off. Chloe turned, pausing when she heard her name.

"I'd like to talk about last night," Aunt Larry said. "Not

right this minute, but sometime today. Okay, Chloe?"

"Okay," she agreed. "Aunt Larry… " She paused, worried if she said anything she would spill everything.

"Have a good time," her aunt said. "Oh, here, wait a minute." She fished through a jar next to her and slid a twenty-dollar bill across the desk. "Just in case you see something you like. And I'm not opposed to treats," she finished with a wink.

Chloe smiled, grateful yet again that she had Aunt Larry. When she picked up the bill, she leaned over and hugged her aunt around the neck.

"Thanks," she said.

"You can tell me anything, Chloe," Larry said. "Anything. Okay?"

Chloe nodded as a car horn honked twice from the front door.

"See you," she said.

Chloe found Marsh in the back seat of the MacKenzies' dark blue minivan. Chloe climbed in beside him to Mary's smiling face.

"Ready?" she asked.

"Ready," Marsh and Chloe replied in unison.

Chapter Twenty-Two

The drive to Charlottetown was informative as Marsh, leaning over to her despite his mother's repeated requests for him to sit back and tighten his seatbelt, filled her in on who owned what field or barn or house for the first ten kilometres or so, then flooded the silence with weird facts about PEI that she didn't know and never wanted to. Mary laughed out loud at him, though, so it was fun even with his endless chatter.

Chloe was unimpressed by Charlottetown, not because it wasn't pretty (it was), but because to her a city was something the size of Ottawa. When they drove over the four-lane bridge across the Hillsborough River, she was surprised they had arrived. The skyline was so much lower than she was used to, houses and condominiums lining the street that ran along the water's edge toward the heart of the capital. Sailboats bobbed in the harbour, bright colours shining in the morning sun.

Marsh pointed out Great George Street and proudly proclaimed that it was the road that the founding fathers walked on their way to the Charlottetown Conference in 1864 when Canada was on the way to becoming a nation. Chloe was impressed by that and tried to muster up more enthusiasm.

The old brick and stone buildings at least felt familiar, but in miniature to what she was used to. When Mary pulled up in front of Province House to let them out, and Marsh told her what it was, she was surprised. Parliament Hill dominated the centre of Ottawa. This was a single squat building, grey with age, the stones appearing lopsided and ancient. Promising to give her a tour someday, Marsh led her across the way to the archives, Mary calling after that she would be back in an hour.

Chloe followed Marsh past the flower-bordered fountain to the tall red brick building next to Province House. Here at least the old trees spread their canopy in a more familiar way, blocking out most of the sun. Despite that fact, however, the day was bright and warm, so the cool quiet of the archive building was a shock. When Chloe climbed the last wide step and walked through the big glass doors, she felt like an intruder. There was something very imposing about the place. Marsh told her it used to be the old courthouse. Chloe felt guilty right away. It was so still and silent inside. Even normal sounds were muffled, like they were wrapped in cotton and happening far away. On the fourth floor, she followed

Marsh with some hesitation to the counter, trying not to touch anything.

A young woman with a blonde ponytail and bright red glasses smiled at them from behind the desk.

"Can I help you?"

"I'd like to see some microfiche, please." Chloe thought Marsh sounded very official, like he knew what he was doing after all.

She seemed taken aback by his request and laughed. "Doing some research?" She was examining them both. Chloe had a moment of panic. What if she said no? Maybe they were too young, or they were in the wrong place.

Marsh, however, knew what to say.

"I was here in May," he said, "with my class. It was awesome!"

The woman laughed, adjusting her glasses. "It was, was it? And you're back for more?" Marsh bobbed a quick nod. She hesitated one more moment before sliding a piece of paper to him. "Good for you. You know what to do?"

Marsh took the pen and filled out the form. Chloe tried to stay quiet and out of the way. When he was done, the woman checked the card. Her eyebrows raised.

"World War II, is it? I'll be right back."

Chloe exhaled, not realizing until then she had been holding her breath. Marsh grinned at her.

"No sweat," he said.

It took the young woman a minute to return with a black box. "Here you are, then, July 1 to September 30,

1941." She came out from behind the desk. "Right this way."

They followed her to a small desk with a box-like reader attached. She removed the two reels of thin film from the case and inserted them into the reader.

"This button goes forward, this one back," she showed them. Marsh was nodding. "Please be careful with the machine, and good luck."

Chloe waited for her to leave before pulling up a spare chair beside Marsh. He shot her an excited grin and started scanning.

It didn't take long for Marsh to find what they were looking for.

"Here it is!" he said. Chloe leaned in for a closer look while he read aloud.

"Joshua Robert MacKenzie, 10. Late of Point Prim, beloved son of Robert William MacKenzie and Margaret Jane MacKenzie (ne. Johnson). Leaves behind sister Mary Margaret, brother Albert Owen, brother Harold Curtis, (twin) brother Joseph Jonathan, sister Emily Anne, sister Emma Pearl." The rest told where he was buried and where he died, but not how.

"Guess it won't be as easy as I thought," Marsh admitted. He scrolled back through the paper to the news section and started scanning.

Chloe, meanwhile, was making connections. "Joseph," she whispered. "Is it the same Joseph, do you think?"

Marsh shrugged, concentrating, then turned to her in shock as he realized what she said. "I bet it is!" He slumped into his seat. "Wow, imagine. His twin." He shook his head and went back to work. "We need to find out what happened."

Finding nothing about it in that day's paper, Marsh went back two more days. "Day for a wake, then the funeral," he told her. "And... here we go! Oh no." Marsh's face fell. "This is awful, Chloe."

She agreed. It was a small story, one brief paragraph. The headline stared at her in bold at the bottom corner of the third page.

> TEN-YEAR-OLD FALLS TO DEATH
> Joshua MacKenzie died late yesterday afternoon when he fell from the loft of his father's barn, striking his head on a support beam. The only witness, his twin brother, Joseph, said they were playing by jumping into the fresh hay when his brother slipped. Authorities have ruled the death an accident.

Chloe's heart constricted. A horrible fear was growing inside her.

"They had a fight," she hissed at Marsh. "The brothers. Joshua wrote about it in his journal. The same day, Marsh. Something about a missing yo-yo. Joshua said that his brother was mad at him."

"What are you saying?" he hissed back. "This says the police thought it was an accident."

"Joseph was the only witness," she told him as his eyes

widened. "What do you think he would have said? 'Oops, I pushed my brother, sorry'?" Chloe felt anger begin to rise for Joshua. She was sure she was right. "That's why he's still hanging around," she said. "His murderer is free and alive and he's dead. All because of a stupid toy."

"We don't know that," Marsh said, trying to calm her down. "Maybe it was an accident."

"Then you tell me what he wants," she shot back.

Marsh couldn't answer.

"I'm going to go see Joseph," Chloe told him, mind made up. Joseph needed to face what he had done, even if he didn't want to. Chloe was determined to make him pay.

"Hang on a second," Marsh said. "We can't just go marching up to his door and accuse him of murdering his brother."

"Why not?" she demanded. Chloe got to her feet, too worked up to sit still any longer. "He did, didn't he? Someone needs to be held accountable." She felt tears rising in her eyes. "He needs to admit what he did."

Marsh shot a look at the lady with the red glasses. She was frowning at them.

"We could call the police?" he suggested.

"Right," she snorted. "Like they would believe us. 'How do we know he killed his brother, officer? His ghost told us!' Great thinking, Marsh."

"Chloe... " His eyes pleaded with her. "What if he didn't do it?"

"What if he did? I need to find out. I'm going to talk to him."

Marsh was squirming now. "But, he's... you know... scary. You saw that shotgun he had! He'll yell at us and call our parents."

"You didn't seem to care so much last night," Chloe challenged him.

Marsh hesitated and dropped his eyes. "That was different," he said, voice hushed. "I don't want to get in trouble."

The woman appeared beside them. "Are you finished?" she asked, looking anxious. Chloe scowled at Marsh. He wouldn't meet her eyes.

"Yes, I guess we are," she said.

It was a long and silent ride home.

Chapter Twenty-Three

Chloe was in the house and running to her room before Mary could get the van backed up and turned around in the driveway. She heard the van pull away at the same time Aunt Larry's office door opened, her voice calling Chloe's name. She ignored her aunt and slammed her way into her room, throwing herself on the bed. She was so furious with Marsh and so wrapped up in the betrayal of Joseph and Joshua that she didn't hear Aunt Larry until she was at the door.

"Chloe!" Her aunt's voice was almost a shout. "What's going on?"

"Nothing!" she yelled back.

"Chloe, open this door right now." Aunt Larry was not impressed. "You can't come barging into the house slamming doors and being impolite. What happened?"

"I don't want to talk about it," Chloe answered. "Leave me alone!"

Aunt Larry was so quiet for so long that Chloe thought she had left until she spoke again. Her voice was very deep and sounded like Patrick's did when her dad was trying to keep his temper.

"We need to make this work for both of us, Chloe," she said. "I may not know much about kids, but I do know common courtesy at any age is to respect others. I'm getting tired of being shut out and talked to like I'm not important. You are very important to me, honey. But you need to talk to me sometime."

Chloe didn't respond. She didn't care. All that mattered was Joshua.

After another long pause, she heard her aunt sigh.

"I didn't want to do this. In fact I swore I wouldn't. I know you're going through a lot but you need to learn some manners, young lady. From this moment you are grounded. No leaving the house for a week. No Marsh, no beach. You can go in the garden, but that's it. Are we clear? Chloe?"

"Fine!" Chloe yelled at her.

"Lunch is ready." Aunt Larry's voice was subdued.

"I'm not hungry," Chloe told the door between them.

Aunt Larry left without another word, but Chloe could hear her start to say bad words when she was halfway down the stairs. She reminded Chloe so much of her dad that she wanted to cry.

Now that she was grounded, she wouldn't be able to

confront Joseph, either. Chloe collapsed on her bed with the journal in her hands. This wasn't how it was supposed to go. She was supposed to rescue Joshua, set him free. It wasn't fair.

Chloe refused to go down to dinner that night as well, but did eat the food that Aunt Larry left for her on a tray outside her door. She waited a long time, dozing now and then, for night to fall. She jerked awake at one point, disoriented. The clock on her vanity said 2:13. Slipping out of her sneakers, Chloe crept to her door and listened. The house was silent. Determined to find out what Joshua had been doing the night before, she snuck out and down the stairs.

Chloe was extra careful. She peeked around the corner at her aunt's door. She could hear faint snoring and knew Aunt Larry was asleep. Being as quiet as she could, now accustomed to the creaking places on the landing and stairs, Chloe wound her way past the noisy boards and to the main floor. Once there, she flew to the little stairway, tripping on her socks as they slipped over the worn treads.

Panting, Chloe paused at the top. The room was empty and quiet, with no sign of the ghost boy.

"Joshua!" She whispered his name into the black. "It's me! I'm here. I know everything, Joshua, about the fall and Joseph. I know what he did. I'm going to make sure he pays for what he did to you."

The boy appeared so close to her, she gasped. He looked even sadder than ever. Chloe reached out to him, but paused when he moved. He pointed to the far corner, near the floor. Chloe followed his gesture then nodded.

"He'll be punished, I promise," she said.

Joshua was crying without sound, shaking his head. He continued to point. Then, he vanished.

Chloe went to the spot and switched on her flashlight. She felt around the floorboards but found nothing. Frustrated, she sat back on her heels. As she did, her eyes drifted slightly upward. She shone her light on the wall, noticing for the first time that one of the panels, the one in the corner, was raised at the bottom. She dug at it with her fingernails and felt that it was loose, but couldn't get it to budge.

She ran back downstairs and to the kitchen. At the last second, she slowed and slid, rather than jerked, open the cutlery drawer. She pulled out a butter knife. Then she raced back to the room.

On her knees, she propped the flashlight against her leg and dug the knife into the gap between the boards. The corner one rocked. She wiggled the knife, trying to pull it loose. The board was stuck and needed a lot of prying. It popped off all at once, clattering to the floor. Chloe froze, listening for her aunt. The house remained quiet. Chloe set down the knife and aimed her flashlight into the hole she had made.

Resting within it was an old wooden box. She reached into the wall and pulled it out. It was yellow. On the top was some worn writing she couldn't read. The box was warped but was held shut by two lengths of some kind of twine. Chloe used the edge of the knife and they parted without effort. Eager for the clues inside, she flipped the box open.

On the top she found a photo. At first she was confused. This wasn't Joshua. The young man was dressed in some kind of uniform. The photo was damaged, yellow with age. She flipped it over. She couldn't make out the writing on the back so she set it aside.

Underneath the photo were various bits of girl treasure. A pin with a rusting flower attached. A bow of some kind of velvet that crumbled when she touched it. But, most important of all, on the bottom under the decay of seventy years of harsh Island winters, lay a small round toy with string hanging from it. Chloe lifted the golden yo-yo out of the box with great reverence. It was cracked on both sides, the old wood shrunken but still intact. The string seemed made of tougher stuff than the ribbon. Chloe gave the loop on the end an experimental tug. It held.

Chloe tried to still the rapid beating of her heart. The yo-yo! She knew how important it was. In her eyes it was the last piece of the puzzle. And seeing as it was in the possession of someone much more feminine than Joshua, she knew beyond a shadow of a doubt that he had been falsely accused.

More determined than ever to make sure Joseph was brought to justice for the murder of his brother, Chloe put all but the yo-yo back in the box and, carrying both with her, retreated back to her room.

Chapter Twenty-Four

Chloe wasn't sure how she was going to get past Aunt Larry the next morning, but she knew she needed to. According to the calendar, it was seventy years to the day since Joshua had died. She didn't know why it was so important that she see Joseph that day, but somehow she knew it was.

She was still racking her brain for a way to sneak out when there was a soft knock on her door.

"I'm going out for the morning," Aunt Larry said. "You don't have to stay in your room, but I expect you to be here when I get back." Her retreating feet didn't wait for an answer.

Chloe sat on her bed, heart pounding as she listened to the sound of her aunt leaving. It was perfect! Of course, she suffered a twinge at once again being forced to deceive Larry, but when her task was done, Joshua would be free and she wouldn't have to do any more sneaking around.

That thought made her pause. Joshua would be free. Which meant her new ghostly friend would be gone from her life forever. It made Chloe want to cry. But, as selfish as she wished she could be, Chloe knew what she had to do.

Before long she was marching with determination across the yard and through the field to Joseph's fence. It wasn't until she was almost there that she spotted a familiar figure waiting for her. Chloe slowed her pace, coming to a halt in front of Marsh. His grin was sheepish.

"Larry said you were grounded." He looked guilty.

"I am," she admitted.

"Figured you'd be along anyway," he said.

"I'm going, so don't try to stop me," Chloe answered.

"I know. I couldn't let you go alone." He beamed his smile at her. "You're way too much fun."

Chloe was glad he was there. "Thanks, Marsh."

Together, they climbed the fence and headed for the cottage. They made it all the way to the front door with no sign of Joseph. Now that she was there at his door, Chloe was afraid. Marsh had been right about the shotgun. And now that she knew, or thought she knew, what had happened to Joshua, she was worried the old man might not think twice about getting rid of two kids who knew his secret. She was about to call the whole thing off when Marsh stepped up and knocked on the door, sealing their fate.

She could hear movement inside, a shuffling step, before the door opened and Joseph was there. He scowled down on Chloe and Marsh, face getting red right away.

"What do you want?" he demanded. "Won't buy no damned cookies or magazines, don't have no bottles or nothin'. Now git!"

Marsh had shrunk back the moment Joseph started yelling, but Chloe got angry. Instead of answering him, she handed him the yellow box.

"What's this?" he grumbled. He stared at it for a long moment, setting his cane aside to turn it over in his large hands. Chloe held her breath, silent. Marsh stared at her, his face a big question mark, but Chloe gave a tiny shake of her head to silence him while she waited for Joseph's response.

It took a while, but Joseph seemed at last to recognize the box, the red in his face fading to pale, pale white.

"Margaret's treasure box," he said, voice barely a whisper. "Where did you get this?" he asked.

Again, instead of speaking, Chloe held out her hand and opened her fingers. The yo-yo glowed golden in the morning sun.

Joseph let out a great breath and sagged against the doorframe. He seemed reduced and no longer frightening at all. He was just a sad old man. He reached out and took the toy. Chloe was shocked to see tears rise in the old man's faded blue eyes.

"You found it," he whispered. "Where did you find it?"

Chloe felt her anger melting and had to force herself to remember why they were there.

"In the old part of the house." She shuffled her feet, knowing she had to share the rest. "I found an old diary," she said, "in a cubby above the stairs."

Joseph's shoulders slumped even further.

"Come in," he said. He clutched the box and the yo-yo in one big hand and retrieved his cane in the other, gripping it tightly as he turned into the house.

Chloe was surprised by his change of attitude, so much so that she accepted his invitation without thinking. Marsh followed along behind her, his mouth open. They found themselves in a small living room with a cramped kitchen attached. The carpet was very old and faded with several spots that looked like they would never come out. The air smelled like onions. Chloe wrinkled her nose and tried to inhale in shallow breaths. The room was quite warm, the dusty windows all shut. The walls were covered in old wooden panelling, the same stuff she had seen in Marsh's house. A small television sat on a rickety table across from a worn and sagging recliner. She watched as Joseph made his way to the recliner and collapsed in it, his cane set to rest on the arm as he laid the box and the yo-yo in his lap.

He looked up at them and motioned with one hand. "There's chairs. Pull up a seat."

Chloe turned, but Marsh was way ahead of her. She sat on the edge of the wobbly old wooden chair he provided her, and he perched on its double. Chloe noticed a bunch of photographs on the wall behind Joseph. None of them were recent. She was too far away to see details, but she knew one of the boys in the family portrait was Joshua.

She felt very sad all of a sudden, her anger at Joseph fading away in the face of how he lived. He looked so forlorn with the simple toy in his big, weathered hands that she forgot to be mad. Still, she needed to know the truth.

"I saved for months to buy this, you know." Joseph's voice was very deep and very soft in the quiet dimness of the room. Chloe almost held her breath as he went on. "Saw it at the store and had to have it. But it was wartime and we didn't have much money, when we had any at all. Poppa made me a bargain. If I worked really hard on the farm, did extra chores, he would give me what he could." Joseph slid an old white handkerchief out of his pocket and wiped at his eyes. "I loved this yo-yo."

He looked up, meeting Chloe's eyes, and smiled. It completely changed how he looked. In fact, that simple smile actually made Joseph look kind for once. "Want to see?"

She glanced at Marsh. They both nodded.

Joseph grunted his way to the front of his chair and spun out the string. Then, he wound it up again and set the yo-yo spinning. He laughed. Chloe could almost see the boy he had been.

"Still works," he said. The shrunken toy landed in his hand. He sat back.

"I read the diary," Chloe blurted. Joseph looked up at her, eyes grave. "I know you and Joshua fought about it."

"I thought he took it," Joseph admitted. "I was so sure. We didn't get along much, Joshua and I."

"I know," Chloe said.

"Guess you do," Joseph answered. He set aside the yo-yo so he could open the box. His eyes widened as he lifted out the photo.

"Angus Morrison," he said, flipping it over then back again. "Well, I'll be." He looked in the box, poking about with one finger. "This belonged to Margaret, my oldest sister." He sighed. "She must have taken the yo-yo," he said. "For Angus. She was so sweet on him back then, always going on about him in his uniform and such. Trying to impress him. I guess she stole it to give to him but never got the chance." He looked up at Chloe and Marsh again. "Angus died in France someplace. Never came home again."

Chloe shifted in her seat, uncomfortable. She remembered Marsh telling her about Joseph's dead sister and guessed it was a heartbroken Margaret. The boy in the photo was the reason she was gone. Still, Chloe hadn't come to find out about Margaret or even about the yo-yo. She had one question for Joseph. He must have sensed her impatience because he put the photo and box aside and reached behind him. He took down a picture from the wall and leaned toward her, holding it out. Chloe took it from him. She and Marsh bent over the old photograph as Joseph talked.

"That's Momma and Poppa on the right. Margaret in the back with my older brothers. And there, kneeling in front, that's me. My little sisters, Emily and Emma. And next to Emma... " he trailed off. "That's Joshua."

Chloe's eyes went right to him and stayed there. She knew that face so well by now she had no trouble picking him out, twin and all. She ran her fingers over his face before looking up.

"You killed him," she said.

"I did," Joseph answered.

Chapter Twenty-Five

Chloe was so shocked she couldn't breathe. Marsh was quivering beside her but she ignored him. Her heart was beating so fast she thought it would fly out of her chest altogether.

Joseph had killed Joshua. She was right. And all over a...

"All over a stupid yo-yo." He said what she was thinking, his voice full of bitterness. "My brother died July 14, 1941, seventy years ago to the day, because I thought he was a liar."

Chloe had to breathe. When she did, it seemed to shatter something inside her. "How could you?" she blurted. "He was your twin!"

Joseph was nodding, rocking back and forth in his recliner. "He was so much smarter than I was. Loved books and learning. All I wanted was to farm, like Poppa. Did most of his chores for him, too. Did he write that in his journal?"

Chloe shook her head, scowling, not wanting to admit her beloved Joshua had any faults.

Joseph nodded. "We fought like cats and dogs," he said, a laugh in his voice. "But I loved him, make no mistake." His laugh died away. "I hated him that day, though, I'll admit it. My yo-yo... I had it one day and then it was gone. He had admired it, gotten mad when I hadn't let him try it. I was so sure he had taken it. But when he insisted he hadn't and I saw him writing in that book of his all smug, I wanted to teach him a lesson."

Joseph looked off into the distance, seeing not the room or the dust motes floating in the air or Chloe and Marsh, but the memory of what had happened seventy years ago.

"I lured him to the barn. We had just cut hay and I had helped Poppa stack it inside. There was a nice loose pile of it under the hatch. I loved to jump out of the loft into it. But Joshua... he was afraid of heights." Joseph continued rocking and rocking, the soft swishing sound of it filling the room behind his voice while Chloe shuddered inside, remembering her own fear looking out over the emptiness of the barn's loft hatch. "I badgered him good, told him if he didn't take my yo-yo he would prove it. He would jump." He shook his head, breaking out of the memory. "I went first, to show him. Then stood like a fool and taunted him from below. He was so scared, I could see it. But I didn't care. I wanted him to suffer for what he did. I saw him sway, take a step. Saw his foot slip." Chloe's stomach clenched and she twitched a little, shoving herself back further in her chair as her mind carried her over the edge of the hole.

Joseph had stopped rocking, body rigid. "I knew before he went that it was bad. But I was down below, out of the way, and couldn't save him." His eyes were full of tears again but he made no effort to use his handkerchief. "He fell and hit his head. I heard the crack of it, like a rock being snapped in half. I ran to him but it was too late. He was already gone." Tears tracked down his cheeks. "And it was all my fault."

Chloe's heart was so sore she was sure it was breaking. She believed him, not because he was so genuine, but because she knew how he felt. The hard knot inside her that had started when the police officer had come to the door grew tighter and tighter. Chloe felt like someone was standing on her chest. She couldn't catch her breath. A huge pain filled her up so completely that she wanted to die.

"It wasn't your fault," she wailed. "It wasn't! It was an accident!"

And then, she started to sob. She sobbed and sobbed so hard that Marsh had to put his arm around her shoulder and hold her to keep her from crumpling. She didn't know how long she poured her heart out but when she was done, the knot was gone.

Joseph reached out and patted her knee. She met his

eyes and they smiled at each other.

"Thank you," he said, wiping tears from his own face.

"You're welcome," she answered.

"And thank you for bringing these to me. The journal?"

"I'll bring it over," she said.

"You keep it," he told her. "But I'd like to see it sometime, if you don't mind."

Chloe nodded.

Chloe and Marsh made a slow walk home after Joseph led them to the door, telling them they were welcome to visit any time. She wasn't sure what to say to her friend and was grateful he stayed quiet.

When they reached Larry's property, Chloe saw the hatchback in the driveway. Aunt Larry was home. Chloe turned to Marsh and hugged him. He hugged her back.

"Think he's gone now?" he whispered into her hair.

"I hope so," she answered.

He exhaled with such heaviness his whole body rose and fell from it. "The rest of the summer is going to be a total bore," he complained.

Chloe laughed.

"I almost forgot!" Marsh dug around inside his pocket for a bit, face excited. "I have something for you." He fished out a shining length of silver and held it out to her. Chloe cupped her bracelet in her hand, feeling it slither into a ball in her palm as he let it go.

"Dad found it by accident. It was in the bottom of one of the buckets when he went to feed the cows. Lucky, huh?"

Chloe smiled at him, her heart so full she could have kissed him.

"Yeah," she whispered. "Thanks." She slid the bracelet over her wrist and did up the clasp. It hugged her like it was happy to be back.

Marsh grinned at her and headed for home. Her last view of him before going inside was a glance over his shoulder and a wave. She waved back.

Chloe heard Aunt Larry in the kitchen and went right to her. Before her aunt could say anything, however, Chloe hugged her.

"I'm sorry," she said, "for everything. I've just been so sad. If you have time, I'd like to talk about it."

Chloe read the last line of Anne of Green Gables and closed the book, hugging it to her as she curled up inside her tent and stared at the photograph of her parents. She brought the crumpled picture to her lips and kissed them both.

"I love you," she whispered, voice still hoarse from crying with Aunt Larry. "I miss you so much. I always will. I felt bad about everything. I was so sure it was my fault. But I know it wasn't. It was an accident, a stupid accident." She set the book down, fingers stroking over the cover. "I just want you to know, I'm going to be okay. I wish you were here, I'd do anything if you would just come back. But it's all right. I know you can't. And that's not your fault."

She heard his sigh and felt him sit down beside her. Surprised he was still in the house, she pulled back the covers to see Joshua next to her on the bed. She was so sure he was gone. Had she missed something?

Then, she understood. Joshua wasn't there for himself. He was there for her. He was smiling. Chloe smiled back. With a gentle wave, he faded away.

"Thank you, Joshua," she whispered. "For everything. I'll take good care of Joseph for you, I promise."

Chloe got out of bed. She took the journal and tucked the photo of her parents inside. She padded to her vanity and opened the brown wooden box Aunt Larry had found for her. With love and careful gentleness, she placed the book, the pencil stub, her bracelet, and her mom and dad inside before closing the lid and going back to bed.

All books are an intense labour of love, and this one was no different.

I couldn't have done this without the support of my darling husband, Scott, who always says yes, no matter how hair-brained the scheme. Much thanks to my mother, Dianne, for loving everything I write and calling me on the parts she doesn't. My beautiful and talented sisters Cat and Caron, my biggest cheerleaders, you must know the feeling is mutual. To my wonderful friends and fellow writers who make this career a joy: Valerie Bellamy, Renee Laprise, Kirstin Lund, Colleen McKie, Annetta Ribken, Joseph Paul Haines, Helen Yee, Lori Whitwam, TG Ayer, Kim Koning and Kimberly Kinrade. Huge gratitude to Terrilee Bulger and Marianne Ward for turning Chloe's story into something we're all proud of.

And the biggest mention of all goes to my dad, who couldn't stay to see my dream come true. Thank you for the typewriter—and the confidence to do something with it.